MOONSTRUCK WITCH

MISS MATCHED MIDLIFE DATING AGENCY
BOOK FOUR

DEANNA CHASE

ABOUT THIS BOOK

A Paranormal Women's Fiction novel.

Midlife isn't for the weak. All Marion Matched wanted to do when she moved to Premonition Pointe was open her matchmaking business and start to relax a little, take morning walks on the beach, and maybe find a hobby or two. Now she's busier than ever, running a successful business and working with her sister for the Magical Task Force, fighting off evil forces.

Marion is just about to head off for a much-earned vacation with her boyfriend Jax, when she gets the call that a string of men who've used her service have been poisoned. And the main suspect is her newest client, the owner of Groveland Farms. With her reputation and business on the line, Marion, and her sister Charlotte, are now on the hunt to find the real perpetrator before they both lose everything they've worked so hard for.

CHAPTER 1

"*Marion!* You dirty little sex fiend," Charlotte said, holding up a very sexy, red, satin-and-lace bodysuit. It had a built-in pushup bra and attached garter belts. "This is so steamy it's giving me a hot flash."

There were so many things wrong with my sister's statement that I hardly knew where to start. "First of all, you're way too young for a hot flash. And second, we both know that little red number isn't mine," I said, shaking my head in exasperation. "It's yours. You bought it last month during that launch party Lennon Love hosted for her new intimates line, Love Me Wild."

"It's mine?" Charlotte asked, holding the garment up to her body. She stared down at it before her lips curved into a devilish smile. "Oh, good. That means *I'm* the dirty little sex fiend. Thank the gods. I was starting to think my geriatric sister was having more fun than me."

"Geriatric?" I screeched, giving her a look of horror.

How dare she? "You did *not* just say that. Take it back, or you're about to be homeless."

Charlotte threw her head back and laughed. "Please. You aren't going to throw me out. Who would take care of your garden while you're on vacation *not* being a dirty little sex fiend?"

"I'm certain I can get Ty and Kennedy to water my plants while I'm gone." I said. Ty was the young man I thought of as a son, and Kennedy was his partner. They were living in the garage apartment. I stared Charlotte down and sniffed, pretending extreme offense. We had that sisterly bond which meant we could get away with saying things to each other that would be completely out-of-bounds if someone else dared to say them. I also suspected that because Charlotte was two decades younger than I was and we hadn't grown up together, we were making up for lost time in the bickering department. At least we were mature enough to handle it with humor… most of the time.

"Oh, come on, Marion," my sister said sweetly. "You know I'm just teasing. You have at least a couple of years before you're ready for the old folks home."

I threw a pillow right at her head.

Charlotte let out a shriek and dove onto the bed, causing the pillow to fly right by.

Luckily for me, I had HGTV'd my bed with a mountain of pillows, so it was easy for me to continue my assault.

When the fifth pillow pegged her in the head, she put her hands up. "You win! I take it back. With an arm like that, it'll be years before I have to pick out your assisted living place. In fact, it'll probably be you who is finding one for me."

"Finally. Now you're talking sense." I dropped the last pillow and went back to packing.

As soon as I turned my back, one of the pillows flew through the air and bounced off the back of my head. I turned around to see Charlotte, staring me down as if daring me to retaliate. "Are you done? Because I really need to finish packing."

She let out an exaggerated sigh and pushed her long red hair out of her eyes. "I just can't believe you're going on vacation in September."

"Why?" I asked her, pulling my neglected bathing suit out of the drawer. It was a two-piece that my friend Iris had talked me into buying after we'd consumed a bottle of wine. It was red with white polka dots, and it was super cute with high-waisted bottoms that covered my middle-age-pooch belly. But still, I hadn't worn a two-piece since my early thirties. Wearing one as I approached my fifties seemed intimidating at best.

"Because it's September," Charlotte whined, "and arguably the best time of year in Premonition Pointe. And here you are, abandoning me to go to Keating Hollow, some tiny little mountain town up north. I mean, it looks like the only thing to do there is hike. You can do that here," she said, sticking her bottom lip out in an exaggerated pout.

"Keating Hollow is a magical town full of witches. Every shop is enchanted. Plus there's a winery and that brewery that has the best hard cider in the entire state. What's not to love about that? It's hardly just a mountain town." I tilted my head and eyed my sister. I knew this wasn't about Keating Hollow. It was about me leaving. "You know we're only going to be gone for a couple of weeks, right?"

"Two weeks while I'll be running the office all by myself! And what if Brix calls and needs us for something? What are we going to do if you're six hours away and unavailable because you've decided to hike up a mountain?"

"Iris will be around. So will Celia," I said.

"Iris rarely comes into the office anymore. She's busy helping that new witch in town set up her pottery studio. What's her name? Autumn Faye Winters?"

"That's her." Autumn Winters had moved to Premonition Pointe a month ago and hired Iris to help her get her business off the ground.

"Anyway, she's busy with that, and I can't even believe that you said Celia would be around. As if she's ever any help unless it's comic relief," Charlotte said with a huff.

"She is helpful sometimes," I said. "She's good at keeping an eye on people when we need her to. Plus, she's pretty great at finding us eligible bachelors. Her recruiting is off the charts."

"Fine. She's useful for those two things," Charlotte relented. "But not when things go sideways. Didn't you hear her tell Sara Groveland that her dates would go better if she showed more cleavage?"

I winced. Celia had said that, and Sara had been more than a little angry. She went on a rant about respecting women and spewed a whole lecture about sexism. She wasn't wrong; Celia had been way out of line. The difference was that Charlotte and I knew not to take the ghost seriously, while the client didn't know we mostly kept her around for her ghostly abilities and entertainment value. "Yeah. That didn't go well, did it?"

"You can say that again. It took you two hours to calm

4

her down and save the deposit she'd given us," Charlotte said. "If something like that happens while you're not here, I'm going to have to banish Celia."

I raised one eyebrow. "You're going to *banish* Celia? I find that hard to believe." My sister and my ghost were like two peas in a pod sometimes. Both of them were free spirits who were amused by each other's antics.

"Banish her from the office," Charlotte clarified. "She can still pop in and visit me here or when I'm getting hit on by random surfer dudes who think they're the goddess's gift to women everywhere."

"That was kind of her to save you from, what was his name, Matty? Manny? Macky?"

"Motley," she said with a grimace.

"That's right," I said, snapping my fingers. "Motley with the buzz cut. Not the crew cut."

Charlotte shook her head. "You're never going to stop saying that, are you?"

"It's funny. Mötley Crüe. Motley with the crew cut. Get it?"

"I get it. And you're a dorky boomer. Stop it."

"I'm not a boomer," I insisted, offended. "I'm Gen X. Get it straight."

"Boomer," she said again with a smirk. "With dad jokes like that, what do you expect me to say?"

"Anyway," I said, "leave Celia out of it. Call Iris if you need anything, and I'm sure you'll be fine. Plus, Brix said he's working undercover and we likely wouldn't hear from him for a month or so." Brix was the director of the Magical Task Force and had convinced me and Charlotte to work as contractors for him when he needed our help with his cases.

5

A few months ago, Charlotte and I had figured out that when we combined our magic, we were two very powerful witches. Separately, not so much, but together, we were a serious force. Brix had called on us a couple of times during the past two months to help him out. Both occasions had just been to break spells on objects they'd seized, but one was a particularly nasty curse that had sent everyone else to the hospital when they'd tried to break it. Charlotte and I had neutralized it on the first try, and it had been impressive. "If Brix does call," I added, "just call me. We'll figure it out."

Charlotte's nostrils flared as she took in a deep breath. "Fine. But just so you know, I'm gonna need hazard pay for dealing with everything on my own while you're gone."

I laughed. "How about I buy you those new boots you like so much down at Sky's the Limit?"

"Sold!"

Minx chose that moment to tear into my room, barking so loud that it made my ears hurt. The small brown and black chihuahua was wearing red-and-white polka dot dress that looked a lot like my bikini. I couldn't help the laugh that bubbled out from between my lips.

"Are you laughing at my dog, Marion?" my sister asked suspiciously as she scooped Minx into her arms, cuddling her to her chest. The dog instantly stopped barking and gave her mother a kiss on the nose.

"I'm sorry," I said, still smiling at the absurdity that my life had become since my sister walked through my front door earlier this year. "It's just that Minx and I match." I held up the suit.

"That's really cute," she said, her expression turning to

one of interest. "Too bad you've spent all summer not wearing it. You two could have been twins."

"Could have. I dare say Minx looks better in her outfit than I do in mine," I said, wrinkling my nose.

She rolled her eyes. "You're hot. Stop with that crap. I'm sure Jax won't be able to wait to get you out of that thing." She took a deep breath and then stood. "I guess I better go and start working on finding some more matches for Sara Groveland. I can't believe how hard it's been to find quality matches for a woman her age."

Sara was turning sixty this year and owned her own farm just outside of town. We'd already had three mixers and five dates, all of them a disaster. The first one had got up and left when he'd gotten a text from his ex-wife. The second one had picked his nose at the dinner table. The third had grabbed her butt not five minutes after they'd met. The fourth one had barely said two words all through dinner and then asked her to pay the bill because his credit card was declined.

The fifth one, Trace Foster, was the one I'd thought had the most promise. They'd had a great date, right up until he'd gotten pulled over for speeding and then hauled off to jail when the deputy sheriff realized there was a warrant out for his arrest. I'd eventually found out that the warrant was for unpaid parking tickets that Trace hadn't even known about. Apparently, his son had been accumulating them and instead of paying them, he just shoved them in his desk and pretended they didn't exist. I'd tried to get the two of them together again, but Trace had been too embarrassed and Sara had said she needed a break to regroup. That's when Celia had made her fatal error and advised Sara to show more cleavage. Saying that didn't help was an understatement.

"I was thinking we should try something outside the box," I said. "Maybe host a hiking meet up or a winetasting or kayaking. Something that will attract people who are interested in the things that Sara enjoys."

"That's a really good idea," Charlotte said, sounding impressed. "A really, *really* good idea."

My sister had just left the bedroom when my phone rang. I glanced at it and called out to Charlotte, "Speak of the devil!" After hitting Accept, I said, "Sara, Charlotte and I were just talking about you. How do you feel about—"

"Marion," she said, her voice shaking. "I think I need your help."

"Sara? What's wrong? What happened?"

"I need a lawyer, and I don't know who to call."

"For what?" My stomach started to ache with dread. Sara might be a petite woman, but she was no shrinking violet. I knew if she was asking for help she was in serious trouble.

Her voice was barely a whisper when she said, "I've been arrested for attempted murder."

"Attempted murder? Of who?"

She sucked in a breath that got caught on a sob before she forced out, "The men you matched with me."

I blinked, staring blankly at the wall, not quite understanding what she was saying. "The matches I made for you?" I parroted stupidly.

"Yes. They were all poisoned. All five of them. The cops think it was me."

CHAPTER 2

"What do you mean they were poisoned?" Charlotte asked as I called Sebastian Knight, Premonition Pointe's resident attorney. He was also the husband of Gigi Martin, one of my coven mates.

"I have no idea. That's all she said." When the ringing stopped, Sebastian's voice mail instructed me to leave a message and I cursed under my breath. When it beeped, I asked him to call me back as soon as possible.

"I guess this means I don't need to worry about finding her a date this weekend." Charlotte refilled Minx's water dish, acting as if this wasn't a huge disaster.

I pressed my palm to my forehead, trying to stave off the headache that had suddenly formed. "What in the hell are we going to do? I need Iris. We need a PR blitz. Some sort of plan for when this hits the news."

Charlotte frowned at me. "Why are you getting so worked up? You didn't poison anyone."

I stared at her, dumbfounded with my mouth hanging

open. "Seriously? You don't think this is going to sink the agency when people find out that the town matchmaker was setting people up with an attempted murderer?"

"But..." She started and then stopped, her mouth opening and closing like a fish out of water. "How are we to blame? We had no idea she was a serial killer!"

"Oh. My. Goddess," I said as my stomach twisted into knots. "Do you hear how awful that sounds? We pride ourselves on vetting our clients. I do a thorough background check on everyone. If there had been even a hint of foul play, I never would have agreed to work with Sara."

"This is so unfair. You can't be expected to know what someone will do in the future," Charlotte said.

"Of course not, but no matter how you look at it, this does not bode well for the agency." I sat down at the table, trying to collect myself so that I could process what this meant for us and why Sara had called me. "She wouldn't have called me if she was guilty, would she?"

Charlotte grabbed a Pop-Tart and sat next to me with Minx in her lap. "If she is guilty, who knows what's running through her mind. A sane person wouldn't go around poisoning their failed dates."

"A sane person wouldn't curse their dates either," I said pointedly as I stared at her.

She was silent for a long moment. "Yeah. I see your point," she said with a quiet nod. "We probably shouldn't jump to conclusions before we know more."

"That's almost always a good idea." It was on the tip of my tongue to say that people who live in glass houses shouldn't throw stones, but I swallowed the impulse. It wasn't Charlotte's fault that she'd been cursed with black magic that had resulted in her unwittingly cursing every man in the same restaurant where she was attempting a love spell. The curse was broken now, but for a while there, it looked really bad for her. Could Sara have suffered the same sort of fate? No doubt, it was better to wait to form any opinions until I had more information.

The front door opened, and Ty called out, "Marion?"

"We're in here." Needing to do something with my hands, I stood and started pulling baking ingredients out of the cupboards.

A high-pitched bark that sounded like it belonged to Ty's Yorkie echoed through the house. Sure enough, Paris Francine ran into the kitchen, jumped on Charlotte's leg and then ran back out with Minx on her tail.

Ty appeared in the doorway and leaned against the frame, his arms crossed over his chest. His dark hair was sticking up all over the place as if he'd just run his hand through it.

"Hey," I said, "I thought you were headed into town to take Kennedy to lunch today."

"I was... I mean, I am." His eyebrows were pinched in concern. "But I wanted to make sure you were okay first."

"Make sure I'm okay?" I asked, surprised. "Sure, why wouldn't I be?"

He cleared his throat and then grimaced as he pulled his phone out of his back pocket. "I was afraid you hadn't heard yet."

"Are you talking about Sara Groveland?" Charlotte asked. "Because we know she's been accused of going all Henry VIII on her recent dates."

11

"Henry VIII?" he asked.

"You know, how the king just offed all his wives when he was done with them. Sara Groveland was arrested for trying to poison everyone she's dated recently. One has to assume she was just frustrated. Or psychotic. Maybe both." Charlotte shrugged.

"Um, okay," he said, sounding unconvinced by her narrative as he turned to Marion. "Have you seen your social media pages today?"

"No. I was busy packing for my trip with Jax and then I got a call from Sara. She's been arrested and has asked for help. That's all I know." We were supposed to leave that afternoon after Jax got home from work. "What's going on with my social media pages?"

Ty pressed an arrow on the screen and then handed the phone over. "You might want to turn the comments off where you can and just log out of everything else for a while."

I scrolled through my Instagram page, my stomach knotted with tension. On every single post for the past two weeks, there were hate messages that called me a pimp, a menace to society, criminally neglectful, and even some who thought I was a co-conspirator who'd helped Sara poison the men. There were photos of one of the men vomiting and looking very frail while he laid in a hospital bed. It was a full-on attack of everything that had to do with the dating agency.

"Oh my gods," I whispered, my hands shaking. "Everything I've built here over the past year... It's just ruined."

"It's not ruined," my sister admonished. "Don't you even

let yourself think that, Marion Matched. You're the best in the business," she proclaimed. "And you have the track record to prove it."

My phone buzzed. The name on the screen indicated it was my alarm company. "Hello?" I answered immediately.

"Ms. Matched? This is Casey from Pointe Protection. The alarm is going off at 15 Main Street. Are you in the office now?"

"No." My heart started to pound against my ribcage. "No one is there today. Or at least there shouldn't be."

"Would you like us to send a call out to dispatch? They will send a patrol car to check on your property."

"Yes, please. And thank you for the call." I hung up, tossed the mixing bowl of ingredients into the fridge, and then strode into the living room. "I have to go to the office. The alarm is going off."

"I'll come with you," Charlotte said immediately.

"You're not going without me," Ty said, already scooping up Paris Francine. "Let me just put her in her crate in the apartment ,and I'll be right down.

"You don't have to go," I told Ty. "I'm sure it's just a glitch with the alarm system."

He shook his head. "Not after this online campaign against you. Who knows what's happening down there? I'm going. You can't talk me out of it."

I gave him a grateful smile. While I didn't want Ty near anything potentially dangerous, it did make me feel better that there were three of us instead of just me. He was right. With the deluge of online hate, anything could be happening.

"Let's go, Minx," Charlotte said, trying to coax her little

dog into her crate. The chihuahua stood still, staring her down. When Charlotte reached for her, she let out a very low growl. "Oh no, little miss. You're going in your crate, or there's no doggie cupcakes in your future. Do you understand?"

The dog hung her head as if she'd been shamed, but still didn't move.

Charlotte snapped her fingers. "Now, Minx."

The dog very slowly slunk into her crate. Once she was in, she turned, giving us a full view of her backside, making Charlotte chuckle. "I know. You're telling me exactly what you think of me right now. But it's your own fault. The last time I left you out here by yourself, you turned a pair of Marion's underwear into crotchless panties. I know you were proud, but she wasn't super thrilled."

I let out a groan, remembering the day Jax and I walked in to find bits of cotton all over the living room. "Charlotte, can we get going now?"

"I'm ready," my sister said just as she reached into the closet and pulled out my dagger. The magical artifact helped wield our power and channel it wherever we needed it to go.

"Good call," I said with a nod. There was no telling what we were going to walk into.

We found Ty already standing next to my SUV when we got outside.

"You sit in the front, Ty," Charlotte said as she climbed in the back.

With Ty seated next to me, I sped off down the street. The sun was high in the sky, shining down on the churning sea to the west of us. I lowered my window, letting in the fall breeze, and had to admit that Charlotte had a point. September really was the best month in Premonition Pointe. The tourist season had died down, the days were mostly sunny with little fog, and the temperature was warm during the day and slightly cooler at night.

Everything about it was perfect, and on any other day, being near the ocean would have calmed me. But not today.

Not when my business was in trouble.

The drive from my house to downtown wasn't very long, but today it felt like it took five years. Every traffic light was red, and when we came to a stop sign, the person in front of us appeared to be lost as he sat there reading a paper map.

"Hasn't that dude ever heard of Google Maps?" Ty said, just as annoyed as I was.

"Apparently not," I said with a sigh.

Just as I was about to drive around him, the car lurched forward, barely missing another car, and then sped off toward the town square. Taking a calming breath, I tried not to speed, but I lost that battle when I saw a crowd of people gathered in front of my office.

"What are they all doing there?" Charlotte asked from the back seat.

Smoke billowed up from somewhere near the front door, and everyone was chanting something… something I couldn't quite make out.

I quickly pulled to a stop about a block away, not bothering to actually find a parking spot, and peered through the windshield. "What are they saying?"

Ty lowered his own window and tilted his head to the side, listening carefully. After a few seconds, he spoke the words along with the protesters. "Light the match, burn it down. It's time to run Miss Matched out of town."

"Oh no!" Charlotte cried as she jumped out of the SUV. She had the dagger in one hand and her handbag in the other.

Ty and I hurried after her.

"Charlotte, stop!" I called. "Don't you think we should wait for the patrol officer?"

"With this crowd?" She shook her head. "No way. They're going to burn the place down."

"Marion!" a familiar high-pitched female voice called.

"Celia." I spotted her right away. The ghost was a waif of a thing with long blond hair and big Kewpie doll eyes.

"What the hell did you do?" she asked.

"Nothing. It's one of my clients."

"Sara Groveland tried to kill all the dates Marion set up for her," Charlotte supplied helpfully.

"*Allegedly*," I reminded her.

Unfortunately, a few of the nearby protesters heard us and suddenly turned in our direction. One of them must have recognized me, and he shouted, "There she is!"

The chants grew louder, and suddenly the crowd formed a large circle around me, Charlotte, and Ty.

I glanced at the building and finally saw what had tripped the security system. The window to the left of the door was broken as if someone had thrown a brick at it. My heart sank, but at least it wasn't worse.

"Whoa! Hold on just a minute!" Charlotte raised her arms high in the air and lowered them in a pulsing fashion, trying to quiet the crowd. Ty and I quickly joined in, but it was clear that no amount of reasoning was going to get them to listen. Their chants only got louder.

The crowd started to close in on us, and neither the Premonition Pointe police or the fire department were anywhere in sight, even though the fire near my front door seemed to be spreading to the decorative planter boxes.

"Celia," I said. "Can you create a distraction?"

"Like what? Show them my boobs?" the ghost asked.

Sometimes I just wanted to strangle her. Instead of lashing out, I said, "Maybe something a little less lewd? Like fly around and buzz their heads? Make them focus on something other than me for a minute."

"On it." The ghost did exactly as I asked. She stepped into the middle of the circle, raised her arms, and then shot into the air like a rocket.

There was a gasp from the people closest to us, followed by more shrieks when she zoomed around, making them forget to chant as they ducked out of the way.

I grabbed Charlotte's hand and hauled her over to the fire. My eyes burned with frustrated tears when I realized they'd pulled my sign off the building and were burning it.

"Hey! That's the sign," Charlotte cried, spinning around to glare at the crowd who were still under Celia's spell.

"I know. Help me put the fire out," I ordered.

"How?" she asked, glancing around. "There's no water nearby."

I pointed at the fire hydrant that was just a few feet away.

She rolled her eyes. "It's not like we have a fire hose."

"But we do have the dagger!"

She looked down at the blade still in her hand, the one

glowing with magic, and she gave me a sheepish smile. "Right." She held it out to me and I grabbed the hilt. The magic clinging to it instantly turned electric blue. Together, we touched the fire hydrant and I cried, "Bless us with water to quench the fire's thirst!"

Magic swirled around the hydrant one, two, three times before the cap flew off and water spilled from the opening, rushing toward the sign. In just seconds, the fire was out and all that was left was a smoking mess.

"Marion! Charlotte!" Ty cried. "Look out!"

I spun just in time to see a tall, black-haired woman barreling right toward us with a bucket of paint in her hands. Just before the red paint splashed all over us, I jerked Charlotte's hand up and the dagger repelled the paint, sending it right back onto our attacker.

Police sirens filled the air.

Finally, I thought as I watched the protesters run in every direction, pushing and shoving their way through the crowd.

Ty moved to stand beside me, watching the chaos with wide eyes.

We waited until the officer made her way to us.

Officer Matson. I'd met her before when Kennedy had gotten into some trouble a little while back.

"Marion Matched," Matson said. "It looks like you're having a rough day."

I blinked at her. "A rough day? I'd say so." I waved at my office behind me. "Some protesters burned my sign and vandalized my office."

She glanced around at the still fleeing crowd. "What were they protesting?"

"Me, apparently," I said, suddenly feeling very tired.

"I see." She looked down at the fire hydrant that was still spewing water and asked, "Did you do this?"

"Yes. If we hadn't, the building was going to go up in flames," I said impatiently. There had been a time in my life when I hadn't had any problems with the law. I was a law-abiding citizen after all. But over the past few months, I'd been in some tricky situations, one of which had ended up bringing down a bigwig with the Magical Task Force. While some members of law enforcement thought that was a good thing, there were even more who were resentful that I'd stuck my nose where they thought it didn't belong. Now I had as much distrust of them as they did me.

"There could be a fine for tampering with the fire hydrant," she said.

"You have got to be joking. Seriously?" Charlotte asked, her hands on her hips. "That's just stupidity. You should be thanking us, not threatening us with a bill. For fuck's sake. What is wrong with you?"

Matson gave Charlotte an impassive stare. "I don't make the laws, Miss Ray. I just enforce them."

Charlotte and I shared a look. The officer not only knew my name, but she knew Charlotte's too. Did that mean both of us were on the local police's radar?

"Did anyone enter your office?" Matson asked.

"I don't know," I said. "We haven't had time to check it out yet."

The officer moved to the door, gripped the knob, and swung the door open with ease.

I let out a gasp. "The door should be locked. They broke in."

Matson signaled to her partner, who was still sitting in the patrol car. When the man joined her, they quickly pulled out their firearms and burst through the door, demanding anyone inside stand down.

Ty gripped my hand and the three of us stood there, frozen, just waiting to see what would happen next.

It didn't take long for Matson and her partner to emerge. Matson holstered her gun and said, "There is nothing amiss inside. I suggest you kill the alarm. If you have any security footage, be sure to drop it off at the station."

"Wait!" I called as she and her partner strode off to their car.

But neither responded. Just after they jumped back into their vehicle, they turned on the emergency lights and sped off toward the south of town.

"I can't believe that just happened," Ty said, staring after the disappearing car.

"I can," Charlotte said. "In fact, I bet they had something to do with the break-in. They hate that we're more powerful than they are."

Too frustrated to even participate in the conversation, I gritted my teeth and entered my office building to silence the alarm. Once it was off, I glanced around at the work area. Matson was right. Nothing *looked* out of place. After a quick trip upstairs to the break area, I confirmed that space looked untouched as well.

When I emerged from the stairwell back downstairs, I spotted Ty and Charlotte entering the office area.

"A fire truck is here closing up the—" Charlotte froze suddenly and said, "Someone evil has been in here."

CHAPTER 3

"*P*lease, I'm not evil," Celia said with a dismissive wave of her hand. The ghost appeared out of thin air and was sitting on my desk, leaning on one hand with her feet tucked under her.

Charlotte frowned and peered in Celia's direction but didn't seem to be focusing on her. "There's dark energy lingering near your desk, Marion."

"I told you—" Celia started.

"Not you. For eff's sake," Charlotte snapped, "not everything is about you, Celia,"

"Well, I never." Celia slid off the desk and placed her hands on her hips. "You don't need to be rude."

"Celia, please," I said gently as I walked over to my sister. "What's happening, Char? Is there a malevolent spirit in here?"

"No." Charlotte shook her head. "It's leftover energy. I'm telling you, Marion, the cop might have said no one had been in here, but she's wrong. Someone evil was in this office."

"Are you sure? You've never really felt energy like that before," I said tentatively. She looked so freaked out.

"I know I haven't." Her fists were clenched and her brows were pinched. "But this… I just *know*."

I placed a light hand on her arm. Instantly, my stomach began to roil and my skin got clammy as intense unease washed over me, making my skin crawl. She was right. Something evil had been in our building. I snatched my hand back and pressed it against my upset stomach. "We need sage. Immediately."

"No, sage!" Celia insisted. "Not yet."

"Why not?" Charlotte and I said at the exact same time.

"Because you should probably try to identify the energy first," Ty said from his spot near the door.

Damn, I'd forgotten he was even still there. The nausea caused by the dark energy had nearly fried my brain. "You're right. I need to get the coven in here to help us trace the intruder."

"Ty? Marion?" a familiar voice called from the door.

I turned around and spotted Kennedy standing there, worry swimming in his brilliant blue eyes.

"What happened? Why are you being targeted?" He walked into the office, stopping when he reached Ty's side. They entwined their fingers together, and I felt rather than saw some of the tension ease from Ty's body.

"One of my clients has been arrested for poisoning her dates," I said wearily. All I wanted to do was close up the office and leave this day behind us. To go home, finish packing, and hightail it out of town. But this was an emergency. I had to figure out if I should help Sara, and I also needed to deal with the fact that while my business had been humming along nicely, now it was in jeopardy. If those protesters thought we were just going to close up shop and move on, they were in for a serious wakeup call.

"They blame you?" Kennedy asked, his eyes wide with worry.

"Apparently."

Charlotte's face turned white and she started to sway on her feet.

"Whoa," I said, grabbing her arms to steady her. That intense dark energy swept over me again, nearly knocking me over. We both stumbled, but we ran into the desk and it kept us both from crashing to the floor.

"We should get out of here," Charlotte said, her face now turning green as she grimaced.

"Ty, Kennedy... Can you take Charlotte home? I'm going to try to do some damage control before I leave," I said, knowing I needed to check the security footage and make certain that nothing had gone missing.

"I don't feel good about leaving you here alone," Ty said, walking over to me. He glanced back at his boyfriend. "Can you take Charlotte, or do you need to get back to work?"

"Sure, I have an hour break," he said and gave Ty a resigned smile. "I guess that means we'll take a raincheck for lunch."

"I don't need an escort," Charlotte said, even as her knees buckled and she had to grab onto Kennedy to stay upright.

"You do," I insisted. "If not for you, then for me. I don't want to be worried about you while I'm dealing with this." I waved a hand around, indicating the office. "Besides, we came in one car. If you take it, you'd have to come back and get us."

"Fine," Charlotte said with an exaggerated sigh, but I knew it was just an act. The relief in her facial expression was enough for me to know she wasn't nearly as brave as she was pretending to be.

Ty walked over to Kennedy, gave him a kiss on the cheek, and said something about making up for their missed lunch date at dinner.

"Definitely," Kennedy said with a nod and then held his arm out to Charlotte. My sister took it, and without looking back, the pair walked out of the office.

"First things first," I said, reaching for my computer to turn it on.

But before I could touch anything, Ty yelled, "No!"

I froze, staring at him with wide eyes. "What is it?"

"You can't touch that. We need to get everything fingerprinted first," he said, striding over to me. "If there's a decent print, you don't want to mess it up with one of yours."

"Dammit." I pressed a hand to my forehead, already feeling a tension headache forming. "But I have to check the security footage, and the only way to do that is on my computer."

Ty bit down on his bottom lip as he contemplated the dilemma. "Do you have any gloves? Isn't that what they use in the detective shows when trying to preserve evidence?"

"Yeah, they do." I walked over to the supply cabinet and instead of using the knob, I carefully pulled the door open from the top, figuring that whoever had broken in hadn't been interested in looking for the extra coffee grounds and paper supplies. I reached in and grabbed a pair of rubber gloves. "This is the best I can do."

"It's better than nothing, right?" he said with a shrug.

"Right." After I had a glove on my right hand, I reached to press the power button on my keyboard, but instead of the computer taking a moment to power up, the screen came up immediately and there was no password screen, indicating that I was already logged in. I sucked in a sharp breath and cursed. Loudly.

"What is it?" Ty asked, rushing over to stand next to me.

"I always, *always* turn my computer off at the end of the day." I waved frantically at the computer. "It was just asleep instead of powered down, which means someone hacked into it."

"Fuck," he said, echoing my earlier curse.

"Exactly." I quickly went to my security website to check the footage and wasn't at all surprised when there was nothing there. The cameras hadn't even recorded us when we'd entered earlier. The system was completely down. The latest video was from the day before when I'd locked up just after five in the evening.

"Should we call the police again?" Ty asked, his eyes full of worry.

I shook my head slowly. When I thought of bringing the Premonition Pointe police in to investigate whatever was going on here, everything inside of me screamed that it was a bad idea. Something was seriously off, and it felt paranormal. There'd been a time when I wouldn't have hesitated to call the Magical Task Force in to deal with the case. But now? After all the corruption they'd had recently, I still didn't trust anyone except Brix. I pulled out my phone and hit Brix's name, already knowing he likely wouldn't be answering. If he was deep undercover, he wouldn't have his personal phone on him. He'd have a new one that didn't have all his Magical Task Force contacts on it. His voice mail greeting started, and the message indicated he was unavailable and to call the office with any emergencies. I left a simple message asking him to get back to me as soon as possible, but I didn't leave any details in case someone was monitoring his phone. My trust issues ran deep.

"This is a job for Sebastian's contacts and the coven," I said and sent a group text to the coven members. One by one they started to reply back, indicating that they were on their way. All six of them. My eyes misted with tears before I blinked, clearing them.

I'd always had friends. Trish, Ty's mom, and I had been as close as sisters before she passed. And then there was Tandy. We'd become close after she'd used my matchmaking services. But I'd never really had a group like the coven. The kind that would immediately drop everything and come running, no questions asked, if one of us called. When people talked about found families, that's what it looked like. At least to me, anyway.

"Marion?" Ty asked, his tone sounding concerned. "What's wrong?"

I jerked my head up and glanced over at him. He was also found family. The young man I thought of as a son had come to live with me after Trish died in a car accident five years ago. There wasn't anything I wouldn't do for him, and I knew the feeling was mutual. "Just overwhelmed a bit, I think. The coven is on their way."

CHAPTER 4

"Sebastian?" I said into the phone, answering it on the first ring.

"Marion," my friend said, sounding concerned. It wasn't the friendly tone I was used to from the resident lawyer. He sounded businesslike and to the point. "Are you all right?"

"I think so," I said with a sigh. "My day has gone up in flames, and my business might be, too. But everyone is safe, so it could be worse, I guess." That was certainly true. No one had tried to harm any of my loved ones. I made a mental note to check on the five men who'd been poisoned.

"I saw the commotion at your office on the local news. They also said something about a fire. What exactly is going on down there?" he asked.

I gave him a rundown of the protest outside of my office and the fire we'd put out. Then I took a deep breath and added, "There's more though."

"There always is," he said gravely.

"One of Premonition Pointe's finest checked out the

office and said everything looked fine. But when we got in here, Charlotte was sort of channeling the energy of someone really toxic. It was so bad that it was making her ill. She's convinced someone was in here. And then when I went to turn on my computer, it was clear someone had hacked into it."

There was the sound of rummaging on the other end of the connection as if Sebastian were looking for something in his desk. "Did you check the security footage?"

"I did. Someone erased it and disabled the feed."

Sebastian let out a grunt of frustration. "Anything else missing?"

I shook my head, even though he couldn't see me. "Nothing's physically missing in the office, but I haven't checked to see if anything else was altered on my computer. Not that they would've needed to delete anything. All they needed was a flash drive if they were looking to steal some of my files."

"Do not do anything else with your computer," Sebastian ordered. "There could be tracking software designed to capture logins and passwords. I want to have my IT guy check it out thoroughly before you access anything sensitive."

Nausea rolled through me. If someone had gained access to my client files, this was a major breach of privacy. When I said as much to Sebastian, he agreed.

"It's a major issue, Marion. I'm not going to lie to you about that. But let us figure out what actually happened before you notify any clients."

"If anyone's personal information was accessed, I have a

duty to tell my clients right away," I said, the tension in my shoulders now traveling up my neck.

"You do. But right now, I'm talking to you as your lawyer. Trust me. You don't want to do anything until we've verified there's an issue and have taken steps to fix it. Then you can release a statement. One vetted by me, understand? The last thing you need right now is a lawsuit. Let's dot the i's and cross the t's before we do anything, okay?"

It didn't feel right to me, but I knew Sebastian was just looking out for my best interests. "If you say so."

"I'm going to send a team over now to dust the place for prints and look for any forensic evidence that could be used to identify the intruder. Touch as little as possible and leave everything where you found it when you walked in today. In fact, the sooner you leave the better. Understand?"

"Yes. I get that you want the crime scene left untouched, but the coven is on their way. We're going to try to conjure up a deity who will tell us who was here and what they want from me."

There was silence for a long moment. "I can see why you'd want to do that at the office. Just try not to touch anything."

I promised Sebastian we'd do our best, and then Ty and I went to wait for the coven members out front.

Gigi Martin was the first to arrive. The petite woman rushed up, her honey-blond hair flying behind her in the seaside breeze. "Marion," she called, waving her hand. "Why are you out here?" She glanced around, frowning at the leftover destruction.

I relayed Sebastian's instructions.

"I should have known he was already involved," Gigi

said, squeezing my hands. "It's good he's working on it. I swear, that man has more contacts than a CIA agent."

Chuckling, I nodded. "It does seem that way, doesn't it?"

Sebastian was a lawyer who'd had his own issues with the law when he was younger, and he preferred to handle any investigations in house instead of relying on the police to solve cases of clients he represented. It meant he had a lot of resources that most other lawyers did not. Honestly, he'd been a blessing to the Premonition Pointe coven, and to me in particular, over the past few months.

"We're here," Grace Valentine said from behind me.

I turned and spotted the real estate agent with the rest of the coven following her. Grace's auburn hair was pulled up into a loose bun, and she was wearing a chic white suit with sparkly blue stilettos. "Did you just come from a showing?"

She nodded and pulled a fun-size candy bar out of her purse. Before she opened it, she thought better of it and put the chocolate bar away. She pushed her bottom lip out, pouting. "I can't have that sugar neutralizing my ability to cast magic. Plus, I'm on a diet... again. I swear, why is it so damned hard to lose ten pounds?"

"Probably because you keep chocolate bars in your purse," Hope Anderson teased.

Grace rolled her eyes at the event planner and then gave me a quick hug. "I'm so sorry this is happening, Marion, but we'll do our best to get to the bottom of it."

"Does sugar really neutralize your ability to do magic?" I asked, a little bit confused. I'd never heard of such a thing.

"A little. I can still cast with the coven, but it does seem to dim my abilities. It's weird, I know. But it was helpful when I couldn't control my emotions and kept hexing my ex by accident."

"That doesn't really sound like an issue," I said with a laugh, knowing that her ex had really screwed her over.

The entire coven chuckled, including Grace. "You might be right about that," Grace agreed. "But I'd prefer it if my hexes were intentional. That's all."

"Fair," I said with a quick nod and then glanced around at the six witches who'd dropped everything to run to my side. "Are we ready to do this thing?"

Iris Hartsen, the woman who'd helped me get Miss Matched up and running and who still worked with me from time to time, stepped in to stand beside me. Her expression was grim as she asked, "Do you think Sara had anything to do with this?"

The question stopped me short. "I honestly hadn't even considered that." I blinked at Iris. "Why would she do that?"

"I don't know. Maybe to put the focus on someone else instead of her?" Iris grimaced. "I hate to even imagine it, but I think we've all seen too much over the past few years. Too many people have turned out to be bad actors, so now we have to ask those questions."

"You're right. We do," I said with a solemn nod and then shook my head. "I don't know what's going on with Sara, but my gut is saying that she's not involved."

"Gut instinct is important," Carly Preston said, speaking up for the first time. The famous actress had been standing back, taking everything in like she usually did until she had something of substance to offer.

Joy Lansing, another one of Premonition Pointe's

actresses, slipped her arm through Carly's and nodded her agreement. "My gut is rarely wrong."

"Thanks," I said, appreciating their support.

The coven members and Ty followed me into the building and into the office I shared with Charlotte, and Iris when she was working with me. Just before I opened the door, I reminded them to be careful not to touch anything as Sebastian was sending forensic investigators.

"Got it," They chimed in together and then filed in one by one. Ty hung back near the door, giving us space to do what we needed to do.

With the seven of us standing in the middle of the room, I glanced around, double-checking to make sure nothing had changed in the twenty minutes Ty and I had been outside. I had no reason to believe it had. After all, who could've gotten in while I'd been right out front? But when you'd seen a shitshow of paranormal activity like I had over the past year, you just never knew what might happen.

Gigi walked slowly toward the desk with her brow furrowed and a frown on her lips.

"What's wrong, Gigi?" Iris asked, moving to stand beside her coven mate.

"The energy in this room is... off." She tucked a lock of her honey-blond hair behind one ear as she stood in front of my computer. "It's concentrated over here."

"That's where Charlotte felt the dark energy," I said. "I felt it when I touched her hand. It was awful. Does anyone else feel it?"

One by one, the witches in the office shook their heads.

"It's smells a little like rotten orange peels," Hope said

with a tiny shrug of her shoulder. "I figured someone forgot to take out the garbage."

I blinked at her. "Rotten oranges?" Then I took a big whiff and shook my head. "I don't smell that." As I checked all three garbage bins, I asked, "Does anyone else smell it?"

"I don't," Grace said, her heels clicking on the tile floor. "It smells a little like damp earth to me. A little moldy."

"Mold!" I cried, suddenly worried that the building was in a state of decay. "Iris?" I asked, my eyes wide with worry. "Does it always smell like that?"

"No." She shook her head and studied Grace and Hope. "You've both been here before. Did you notice anything smelling off then?"

"Nope. Just today," Hope said.

"I don't think so," Grace added. "And I'm pretty sensitive to that stuff. You'd be amazed at what clients smell in houses I'm showing them. I've kind of honed my sniffer to notice even the faintest scent."

"Thank the gods for that at least," I muttered. "Do you suppose those scents are left over from the intruder?"

"It's probably how they are interpreting the foul energy," Gigi said. She waved at the desk. "The energy is strongest here. I think we should form a circle around your workspace and try to summon a goddess for our answers."

The coven members spread out, each of them stepping into the circle formation, leaving the space in front of the computer for me.

I straightened my shoulders and took my spot as Grace opened a canvas bag and passed out white pillar candles.

"This would be easier if the intruder had left a calling card of some kind," Gigi said. "But since all that's here is their funky energy, how about we try to channel that as we call on the goddess?"

"Sounds like a decent plan," Iris said, placing her candle in front of her on the floor. The rest of the coven followed her lead and then we reached for each other's hands.

"Marion, you lead," Gigi said quietly.

With a quick nod, I closed my eyes and opened myself up to the power of the coven, waiting for the rush of magic that always filled me when we were connected.

But instead of magic flowing through my veins, a wave of nausea washed over me, making my stomach churn.

"Ugh!" Hope cried as everyone else made their displeasure known. "What the hell was that?"

"It's the evil energy that's hanging around in here," Gigi said quietly.

I nodded my agreement. "It's what I felt when I touched Charlotte. She doesn't seem to have any defenses to keep it at bay. It's why I sent her home."

Hope shook herself as if casting off the energy. "How do we block it out so we can do what we need to do?"

"We just need to focus on the magic," Iris said. "Think about that, and it shouldn't affect us that strongly."

"We could try it," Gigi said with a nod.

"Okay," I agreed, already dreading the nausea that was sure to return. "Ready?"

Everyone held their hands out, and as soon as I clasped mine around Gigi's and Hope's, that greasy wave of darkness rippled into me. I squeezed my eyes shut and tried to focus on connecting with the magic of my coven. The negative energy started to dissipate, but I couldn't sense any magic.

Nothing.

No spark whatsoever.

Opening my eyes, I glanced around at the coven members. "What's happening right now?"

"Nothing," Iris said, sounding frustrated.

"My magic is barely sparking," Gigi added.

Hope let out a grunt of irritation. "My magic is MIA."

"Same," Grace said.

Joy and Carly both confirmed they didn't feel anything either.

"It feels like that dark energy is blocking us," Gigi said, dropping Iris's hand and mine. She slowly walked around the circle, shaking her head. "This isn't going to work. Not here. Not until we can do a good cleansing at least."

"I have sage," I said, already walking over to the closet where we kept supplies. "We can do it now."

"No," Gigi said firmly. "Not yet. We don't know exactly what we're dealing with."

I frowned. "Does that matter if all we're trying to do is cleanse the place of the bad energy?"

"Yes," Carly said, answering for her. "If it's a curse, best case scenario, the sage does nothing. Worst case, it unleashes something really ugly that we can't handle. It's better to wait until we know what it is and then form a detailed game plan so no one gets hurt."

If only Charlotte was there with us. Together, when we held my dagger, so far we hadn't come in contact with any spell we couldn't neutralize. Though I agreed with my coven mates that the more information we had the better. "Okay. If our magic won't connect here, what do you suggest? Head to the coven circle?"

"Yes," Gigi said, already moving toward the door.

I let out a frustrated sigh. "I'm sorry. This was a huge waste of time for everyone."

Iris stopped suddenly. "No, it wasn't. We do know one thing."

"What's that?"

"Sara didn't have anything to do with this. Nothing about that dark vibe is related to her energy at all," Iris said with an air of authority.

Iris was right. Nothing about this felt like the woman I'd been working with. "But how do we know if this is related to the poisonings?"

"We don't," Gigi said. "But it would be quite the coincidence if it wasn't, right?"

She had a point. "I guess that means we're going to need to get Sara a lawyer."

Gigi nodded. "I'll call Sebastian on the way to the coven circle."

CHAPTER 5

"*A*re you sure you don't want me to come with you?" Ty asked as I pulled up to my house.

"What would there be for you to do?" I asked, putting the SUV in Park. "It's just a summoning with the coven. Nothing we haven't done before."

"Sure, but…" He shook his head. "I don't know. I was going to say those summonings didn't involve evil energy hanging around your office, but I suppose curses aren't any better."

I placed my hand on his arm reassuringly. "I'm going to be there with six other coven members. Together, we'll be fine. Especially there." The coven circle was where we drew our power, and I'd venture to say that if someone or something attacked us there, they'd be in for a world of hurt.

"I know. I guess I'm just unsettled after everything that happened today." He clasped his hand over mine and squeezed. "I'm allowed to be worried about my mom, right?"

Mom. My heart squeezed with the love that wrapped around it. Ty wasn't my biological son, but since we'd lost his mother, Trish, I'd been there for him in all the ways that a parent would. The fact that he thought of me as his pseudo mom… Well, it was an honor.

I gave him a small smile. "Of course, you're allowed to be worried. The goddess knows I'd be terrified if you were running off to deal with some unknown evil energy. In fact, if anything actually does go wrong while we're at the coven circle, I wouldn't want you anywhere near there. Knowing you're here, safe, means I'll be safer since I won't be worrying about you."

Ty let out a sardonic chuckle. "I see what you did there. It still doesn't make me feel better about staying here, but I get your point."

"Does that mean you're actually going to get out of this vehicle?" I teased.

"When I'm ready," he deadpanned.

I chuckled and then reached across the SUV to give him a hug. "Thank you for being there for me today. But the coven and I have got it from here. Will you go check on Charlotte and text me so that I know she's all right?"

"Sure." He clung to me, holding on tight.

"Ty? Are you okay?"

He let me go and then cleared his throat. "To be honest, I'm not sure. But I will be. Just as soon as you get home from your coven meeting."

In that moment, all I wanted to do was walk into the house and forget this day had ever existed. I wanted to be with my family and reassure them that everything was fine. But it wasn't fine. The day had imploded, and I had no idea what we were dealing with now.

Why couldn't we all just catch a break?

"I'll be back as soon as I can. Hopefully, we'll have answers and can make some sort of plan."

"That would be nice." He forced a smile and then climbed out of the SUV. Just before he shut the door he said, "I don't know why, but I have a really bad feeling about this. So just be careful, okay?"

I gave him a solemn nod.

He pushed the door shut, and I just sat there for a moment, watching as he walked into the house. The fact that Ty had so readily voiced his concerns about the situation unsettled me. He wasn't one to be overly dramatic. That was Charlotte and Celia's MO. For him to say something meant he couldn't shake that feeling. It wasn't something I took lightly.

I glanced into the back of the SUV and spotted my dagger. The sight of it did little to reassure me. There were just too many unanswered questions. With my spine stiffened, I put the SUV into gear and headed to the bluff to join my coven.

"THE ENERGY here couldn't be more different than back at your office, Marion," Gigi said. She took a deep breath, inhaling the sea air.

I followed her lead, letting the salt air cleanse the negative energy from my being. I needed to shake my fears if I was going to be useful in this summoning. Goddesses weren't exactly easy to summon. I had to be at the top of my game.

"I agree," Carly said, stepping up beside Gigi. "The only problem is, we don't have anything to use to identify the intruder. Back at Marion's office, at least their energy was everywhere."

"True." Gigi turned to me. "I think we're going to need you to stand in the middle of the circle."

"Me?" I asked, more than a little shocked by the suggestion. "Why me?"

"Because," the ethereal woman said with a swipe of her hand, "the intruder's energy swept through you when you and Charlotte were at the office. If she were here, I'd ask her, but since she's not, you're it. Unless you want to get her over here."

Frowning, I shook my head. I absolutely did not want to put Charlotte through a goddess summoning. Especially one where the goddess would talk through her. She'd been through enough today already. "No. I'll do it. Charlotte's not really in a place to handle a goddess."

"I figured as much," Gigi said kindly. "Don't worry, Marion. The coven is strong. We'll keep you safe through the entire thing."

An ache formed in my gut. Was this why Ty had been so worried? I hadn't realized they would want to use me as the vessel for the goddess. Opening oneself for something like that was inherently vulnerable. If one thing went wrong, literally anything could happen.

Iris walked over to me and squeezed my hand. "You don't have to do this. You know that, right?"

"Yes," I said automatically, but I didn't mean it. Whatever had entered my office hadn't just invaded my space; it had also made Charlotte so sick that she'd almost passed out. That type of energy wasn't something I could just ignore. If I didn't do something about it, or at least understand what might be coming for us, then we'd be sitting ducks. I couldn't do that to my family. "Thanks for that, but unless anyone has any other ideas about how to figure out what's invaded my life, then I think Gigi is right. I have to do this."

Everyone shook their heads. Normally if we were going to summon a goddess for information about someone, we'd need an object that carried that person's energy. We didn't have anything to go on other than the energy that had been left at my office. If the only way for the goddess to get a sense of who or what we were dealing with was through me, then there was no other option.

"Okay then." I stepped into the middle of the circle. "Let's get this show on the road."

Without a word, my coven mates went to work securing the circle. Hope poured a fresh layer of salt to keep anyone or anything we summoned in the circle.

With me. A small shudder ran through my limbs. I knew a goddess was just about the safest thing we could summon, but when that veil was lowered, sometimes unpredictable things could happen.

Hope passed out the white candles to each of the witches, and then they fanned out, taking their places on the circle. Inside the salt barrier, the faint outline of a pentagram appeared. There was magic already in the air, waiting for the coven to harness it. I shifted to make sure I was in the center of the pentagram and then waited.

41

Gigi took the northern spot on the pentagram and held her arms out wide and let her head drop back so that the midday sun was shining on her face.

The rest of the coven followed.

"Goddess of knowledge, we're here to seek answers," Gigi called.

The wind picked up, circling around me, sending my hair whipping across my face.

"One to seven and seven to one, the coven asks that secrets be undone," Gigi continued.

The candles sitting at the edge of the circle flamed to life.

"Fire, water, earth, and air, we come together to seek your guidance. Air, earth, water, and fire, we ask the elements to bring us truth."

"Air, earth, water, fire," the coven chanted together. "Fire, water, earth, air," they continued, their voices rising over the increasing wind.

Gigi raised her arms straight up in the air and called, "Reveal yourself if you dare!"

My body suddenly became very rigid and my lungs seized. I tried to open my mouth to call out, to cry for help. But I couldn't. I was standing, but I couldn't use my limbs. Couldn't turn my head. Couldn't speak. I couldn't even breathe.

"Goddess of knowledge and power, we seek your wisdom," Gigi continued. "We welcome you into our circle. Show yourself to your humble sisters on earth."

Each of my coven sisters kneeled at the edge of the circle, their gazes turned up as they stared at me, their eyes widening in surprise.

My lungs were burning, and my head started to swim from the lack of oxygen. If it hadn't been for the spell holding me up, I was certain that I'd have already collapsed. My vision started to blur, and somewhere in the back of my mind I started to wonder if I was going to suffocate right there in front of my coven.

My heart ached for Ty and Jax and my father.

Charlotte's face appeared in front of me. *Stop it*, she ordered, her expression pinched in anger. *You're not leaving us just yet, Marion Matched!*

Air suddenly filled my lungs, and my vision cleared. But when I tried to open my mouth to ask what had happened, I heard a voice in my mind. *I'm here now, Marion. Your body is mine... for now.*

Panic flooded my mind, and once again I started to feel lightheaded as I desperately tried to understand what was happening.

But then my mouth opened and words I wasn't speaking came out. "Silence!" my intruder ordered.

It was then that I realized the coven had still been chanting, still summoning the goddess.

"Who are you that you dare to summon me?" the intruder demanded.

"Goddess Athena," Gigi said with a whisper. "We are honored by your presence."

The being—*or goddess*—who had taken over my body, seemed to relax. My limbs were no longer tense, and a small smile claimed my lips.

"I should hope so," the goddess said. "After all, it's very unusual for me to entertain such arrogance. But with a summoning like that…" She let out a bark of laughter. "How could I possibly resist?"

"We are humbled by your generosity," Gigi said, stroking the goddess's ego.

I felt the goddess's pleasure ripple through me. Gigi was handling this exactly right. If there was one thing I knew about goddesses, it was that they demanded respect. And if they didn't get it, there was no telling what they might do.

"What is it you want from me, child?" Athena asked her.

"Your wisdom. Dark energy has entered our lives, but we don't know who it belongs to or why it's suddenly here in our town. We humbly are asking for help to identify the intruder."

"And just how am I supposed to identify this intruder?" Athena asked, sounding more curious than put out now.

"Marion, the vessel you are borrowing, felt their energy through another. Remnants should still remain in her psyche."

"I see," Athena said with a nod. "Does this vessel give me permission to invade her essence?"

No! I cried in my mind. That would mean opening myself up to this goddess to invade every tiny particle of my being. Nothing would be untouched.

"Your vessel is not up for the challenge," Athena said, sounding bored now. "You have wasted my time."

A tiny bit of air filled my lungs, and I could feel the goddess starting to slip away.

"Wait!" I suddenly cried, realizing that our opportunity for getting any answers was quickly slipping away from us. The word came out garbled, and I wasn't even sure I'd been coherent, but the goddess slipped back into place, paralyzing me once again.

"You've had a change of heart?" she asked, sounding unconvinced.

Yes, I thought, bracing myself for whatever happened next.

Immediately, a queasy feeling took over, and then that same darkness that overtook me when I'd touched Charlotte earlier invaded my entire being. Hopelessness and despair pricked my heart, making me want to cry out, but I couldn't. I was just trapped in that pit of darkness.

My mind suddenly filled with memories of my past. Memories I'd buried long ago. The ones I always pushed aside any time they started to creep into my psyche.

My mother leaving us when I was young. My father a shell of himself for weeks, unable to emotionally be there for his daughter, who needed him more than ever. My mother returning with another daughter years later, only to leave again. Me consoling Charlotte when she realized our mother wasn't coming back. When I'd broken things off with Jax because I realized our auras weren't compatible. I'd seen what had happened to my parents and was never going to go through that. The physical pain of my heartbreak that had followed when I'd set him free had almost been more than I could bear. And then there was the devastation that night when I'd gotten word that I'd lost Trish, my best friend.

Athena raised my arms, face tilted toward the warm sun. And then suddenly, my head dropped back as she swayed on my feet. When she jerked my head back up, her voice was as clear as a bell when she said, "The one you seek is hiding in plain sight." Then she widened my eyes and a ripple of pure disgust from the goddess filled my senses. Her voice was low and full of venom when she added, "Beware those who walk under the moonlight."

Suddenly the goddess vanished, leaving me empty and cold as my limp body collapsed to the ground.

CHAPTER 6

"*M*arion," Grace called.

I blinked, unable to focus.

"You're okay, Marion," Iris said, placing her hand on my shoulder.

"Iris?" I blinked again, this time clearing the haze from my vision. "Where are we?" Panic started to well in my chest. I had no recollection of where I was or how I'd gotten there.

"We're at the coven circle on the bluff. Don't you remember?"

I pushed myself up into a seated position and had to grab my head when it swam from the movement.

"Whoa. Just take it slow," Iris soothed.

I peeked at her and then around at the rest of the coven. They were all staring at me, concern radiating from each of their expressions. "I'm fine," I insisted as the wave of dizziness passed.

When no one said anything, I glanced at Grace, noting the pure empathy in her eyes as she gazed down at me.

"Why are you looking at me like—" Before I could even get the rest of the words out, my mind flooded with the memory of the goddess possessing me. The memories that had taken me to my darkest moments. And her warning just before she'd vanished. Taking a deep breath, I forced myself to meet the gazes of each of my coven mates. Every one of them was staring down at me with compassion, and in that moment, I just knew. "You saw it all, didn't you?"

Iris cleared her throat and cautiously said, "We saw the goddess use your body as a vessel if that's what you mean."

"Iris," I said in a flat tone, indicating my minor annoyance. "Don't do that. You know what I meant."

She cleared her throat and glanced away for just a moment before letting her eyes meet mine again. "We saw what she did to you. The memories of your childhood and teen years. Yes."

I let out a groan and rubbed at my face.

"It's a lot," Gigi said. "But if there is anyone you can share that stuff with, it's us. You know that, right?"

"It's what we're here for," Carly added. "It's not all coven circles and herb potions with this coven."

"They're right," Joy said, sitting down next to me in the dirt. "We might be a coven, but we're sisters first."

I rewarded Joy with a smile. I really appreciated what they were doing. But that didn't mean it didn't make me uncomfortable. "Listen, guys, this therapy session is great and all, but can you stop looking at me like I just lost my puppy? All of that was a long time ago, and we all know the goddess just stirred all that stuff up to pilfer my brain and find the energy of the intruder."

"And because she's a power-hungry deity," Hope said with an air of disgust.

I raised my eyebrows at her. "Is this not your first run-in with Athena?"

"No, it is," she said, placing her hands on her hips and flicking her long dark hair back. "But there is no way she needed to scramble your brain like that just to latch onto the energy of the person who broke into your office. Any goddess worth her salt wouldn't have tried to break you first before leaving us a cryptic-ass message to decode. I mean, what in the hell are we supposed to do with 'Beware those who walk under the moonlight?' That could literally mean anyone or anything."

"Don't forget she also said, 'The one you seek is hiding in plain sight,'" Grace said. "If that's the clue, then we have to be suspicious of every person we interact with. Not to mention our families. It puts the whole town under suspicion and is useless as a starting point in any kind of investigation."

Iris sat back on her heels. "Hiding in plain sight probably means the person is someone we trust."

I swallowed the sudden bile in my throat and pressed a cool hand to the back of my neck. "This really does mean we need to consider our friends and family."

"Only the ones who take moonlit walks, apparently," Hope said with a snort.

I couldn't help it. I chuckled. "You have a point. What do we do, put ankle trackers on our friends and family and

49

then wait until they go skyclad on their next walk down by the beach?"

Hope gave me a look that indicated she was considering my suggestion.

Grace elbowed her gently. "None of that. If we followed that plan, your mother would be the first one we'd question."

Hope threw her head back and laughed. "You're not wrong about that." Then the raven-haired beauty sobered as she gave me her full attention. "This was a mistake."

"What was?" I asked, pushing to my feet and groaning when my back ached in protest. Apparently, my almost fifty-year-old body didn't appreciate being thrown on the hard ground.

"This. Calling the goddess and letting her use you to seek out whoever targeted your office. It was far too invasive for far too little information." She glanced around at the other coven members. "Just because we *can* do something, doesn't mean we *should*."

Grace placed a hand over her heart and nodded. "I agree. This was far too painful for very little useful information. We have to do better next time."

The mood of the coven was somber and heavy. All because they'd had to witness my personal traumas. But everyone had something they'd had to go through. It wasn't like some deep dark secret had been revealed that was going to harm me now. I'd already worked through those issues and was fine now. Or as fine as one could be when they'd been abandoned by their mother time and time again. Though, I did see what they were saying. If I'd had darker situations I'd gone through in my past, it could have thrown me into a serious mental health crisis.

Gigi moved to stand next to me, her face ashen as if something devastating had just happened. "I'm so sorry, Marion. This was my idea, and I just didn't realize how invasive that would be. I should've—"

"Wait," I said, throwing my hands up. "Please don't. I really appreciate how caring and empathetic you all are being. And I love you for it. But I'm okay. Really. All that stuff is in the past. Yes, it sucks having it all brought back like that, but I'll be okay. I promise. There's no need to apologize to me. No one forced me to open myself up like that to a goddess. I went in willingly, looking for answers. Would it be nice if we'd gotten anything even remotely useful rather than a cryptic message that could mean just about anything? Sure. The honest truth is that I'm wigged out enough about what happened today that I'd do it again in a heartbeat if I thought it would help."

"But, Marion," Joy said, giving me a troubled look, "I think we're all just saying that a lot of what we do is unpredictable and maybe we should be a little more careful."

"I know. And like I said, I appreciate that. All I'm saying is that I gave consent for this, and I'd do it again. So maybe we think a little more about possible consequences before we jump into the spells and summonings we cast, but we should still respect when a member is ready to dive in with both feet."

"That's fair," Gigi said with a short nod. "There have been times in my life when things have been so dire that I'd have done just about anything to change things, so I see

51

where Marion is coming from. That's the beauty of being part of this coven. When something goes sideways, there's always a trusted group right there to back each of us up."

"I think it's just the nature of wielding magic," I said. "There are risks. That's not new."

"True," Carly said. "Gigi and I run into that all the time when we're making our skincare products. There's always a risk when magic is involved. They only thing we can do is try to understand them so we can avoid harm."

"That's why we test everything on ourselves," Gigi said with a sardonic chuckle. "Remember that time I made that rejuvenating cream and it made my lips swell up to three times their size? I looked like I'd gotten into a fight with a Botox needle and the needle won."

"See?" I said. "We all take risks. This was one I took. I agree that we should probably be a little more cautious in the future, but let's try to let this one go, okay? I'm fine. Or at least I will be when I get some painkillers in me to deal with this back issue." I pressed my hands to my lower back and made a face. "I swear, this getting-older shit sucks."

"Only when it comes to rolling out of bed in the morning," Iris quipped, making us all laugh.

"Too true." I jerked my head toward the trail that led back to the road. "Come on. Let's get out of here before another goddess shows up and decides to pick apart my commitment issues."

There was more chuckling as we all trudged down the path. When I finally slipped into my SUV, I sat there for a few moments, watching as my trusted girlfriends all left one by one. Then when I was alone, I finally succumbed to the tears I'd been holding back and let out an anguished sob.

CHAPTER 7

*F*eeling hollow and wrung out, I finally put the car into gear and drove the short distance to my small cottage a few blocks off the beach. It was dusk, and the lights shone brightly from the front two windows, indicating that Charlotte was home. Once I had the SUV parked in the driveway, I took a moment to check my face in the rearview mirror. There was no hiding my puffy red eyes or my red nose.

"Shit," I muttered. The absolute breakdown I'd had on the side of the road back at the bluff had been a surprise to me. I'd meant everything I'd said to the coven. That all of my baggage was in the past and I'd worked through it. But obviously I hadn't if I'd just had a ten minute crying fest.

I quickly searched my glovebox for a napkin or wet wipe. As if I, a woman nearly in her fifties who'd never had children, actually kept wet wipes on hand. I rolled my eyes at myself and grabbed the one napkin I found and tried to mop up my face. As predicted, it did nothing to hide the mess I'd made of myself, and I forced myself to go inside. If I was lucky, Charlotte would be in the kitchen and I could slip into my bathroom for a minute before anyone saw me.

No such luck.

"Damn," I said very softly when I opened my front door and found not only Charlotte in the living room, but Ty and Kennedy, too.

"Marion?" Ty said, his tone full of concern as he jumped up and ran over to me. "What happened? What's wrong?"

I let out a humorless chuckle. "You mean besides an evil being breaking into my office and all the online chatter about my deadly matchmaking services?" Yeah, after my crying jag I'd made matters worse by going online and reading all the memes and comments that had already been posted about Miss Matched Midlife Dating Agency. The most popular meme was my logo that had been transformed into *Miss Matched Deadly Dating Agency, perfect for assassins and serial killers.*

Ty put his arm around me. "For the love of the goddess, you didn't actually go online, did you?"

I just nodded, ready and willing to let him think that's what had gotten me so upset. It was better than having to explain what had happened at the coven circle.

"Mama Marion," he said, shaking his head and giving me the same sympathetic look I'd gotten from my friends earlier.

"Stop," I said, waving a hand in the air. "I'm fine. Everyone's allowed a breakdown when the stress gets to them, right? In fact, it's better to let it out instead of allowing it to fester. That's all that happened. Now I'm ready to work on figuring out how we can fix this." Without waiting a beat, I turned to Charlotte. "How are you? That negative energy didn't follow you home, did it?"

She shook her head. "No. In fact, as soon as we left the office it was gone." My sister narrowed her eyes, studying me. "What about you? Your energy feels a little... off."

"You can feel my energy?" I asked, more than a little surprised. If she'd been touching me, I'd have understood it because of our magical connection. But at the moment, she was across the room. Charlotte wasn't an empath. She shouldn't have been able to tell what my energy felt like.

"It's just a sense that something's not quite right," she said with a shrug, already rising and moving toward me.

I put up a hand. "Just give me a minute. I need to use the restroom." Quickly, I ducked into my room, saw the open bag I'd been packing earlier, and nearly cried again. Somehow in all of the commotion, I'd forgotten all about my plans with Jax. One glance at the clock told me he was likely on his way and had no idea that our plans had changed. With a sigh, I put my phone down and headed for the shower. There was no point in texting him now. He'd find out soon enough that we weren't going anywhere for the foreseeable future.

With the hot water sluicing over me, I stood in the shower, willing the water to cleanse my battered soul. It had been too much. The call from Sara, the protest, the break-in, and then the emotional bruising from the goddess. Plus knowing that something nefarious was lurking out there, wreaking havoc on our lives. It was enough to make me want to curl up into the fetal position and will it all to go away.

But that wasn't me. It never had been. I wasn't one to put

my head in the sand. If something was off, if someone I loved was in danger, I was always right there, ready to make everything right again.

Today was just a setback. By tomorrow, I'd be ready to kick ass and take names. Just like I always had.

It wasn't long before the bathroom door opened. I knew it was Jax without even looking. And when he slipped into the shower a moment later, he didn't even say a word as he wrapped his arms around me from behind and pressed a soft kiss to my cheek.

I leaned back into him and closed my eyes, desperate for his comforting embrace and grateful to have him back in my life and back in my heart after everything that had happened when we were just kids.

Jax's hold tightened around me as he nuzzled my neck, hugging me to him.

He knew about the day's drama. There was no doubt about that. Well, how could he not? It was all over social media. And likely the gossip about the protest at my office that morning had been at peak levels all over town.

I couldn't remember a time when Jax and I had shared a shower when we hadn't been full of passion for each other. That was one thing that had never changed between us. The chemistry was off the charts. On any other day when Jax joined me in the shower, we'd already be going at it like we hadn't touched each other in months.

But today, he was just here, holding me. Loving me exactly the way I needed him to.

My heart was full of love for this man. The fact that our auras didn't complement each other meant nothing to me now. All that mattered was this deeper connection we had.

The one that made us choose each other over and over and over again, despite not having that initial love match, the one that helped me bring people together every day in my job.

It had been a hard thing for me to swallow. That people could love deeply and completely without that fated invisible string. After years of matching people off their auras and building a successful business using my gift of just knowing when people were a match, it had taken a lot to get me to believe that compatible auras weren't necessary.

And now here I was with the love of my life, feeling like we did have some sort of invisible string holding us together. Maybe we did. Love was just like magic. Unpredictable. Wild. And more powerful than anyone could imagine.

Jax's hands started to roam down my hips and then up my back until they settled on my shoulders. While dropping kisses on the back of my neck, he started to knead my tense muscles.

I leaned back into him, letting him hold me up as my body started to relax for the first time that day.

"I won't tell you it's going to be okay," he whispered in my ear. "We both know no one can promise that when there's a shitstorm brewing. But I can promise you I'm here. Whatever you need, I'm here."

This man. What had I ever done to deserve him? My heart started to pound against my ribcage as I turned and looked up at his handsome face. His dark eyes were trained on mine, compassion shining back at me. No pity. Just love and understanding. I adored him for it. I pressed my hand to his face, caressing his cheekbone. "You have no idea how good it is to see you."

He smiled down at me and brushed his knuckles over my cheek. "I have a pretty good idea."

I let out a choked laugh and shook my head. "You don't know the half of it."

He leaned down, touching my forehead with his as we stood there under the spray just breathing each other in.

There were no words for how much I appreciated him in that moment.

Finally, he pulled away and gently turned me around. Reaching past me, he grabbed a pump of shampoo and then went to work on slowly and meticulously massaging my scalp. My eyelids slid closed as I luxuriated in his touch.

When was the last time I'd felt so cared for? I had no idea. Jax was a wonderful partner, but when we were together, there was usually fire between us. That passion we shared was a vibrant spark that never seemed to dim. It made for a wonderful sex life, but this... The care and tenderness he was showing me was a rare moment for us.

His touch nearly brought tears to my eyes. But after the day I'd had, I was completely cried out. All I wanted to do was curl up in his arms and forget this day ever happened.

After Jax had finished with my hair, he took his time thoroughly washing every inch of my body. His touch was tender and sure, and by the time he was done, I was so pliable that I let him guide me out of the shower and dry me off. When he reached for my favorite nightshirt, I put my hand out to stop him.

"No. I don't want anything between us tonight," I said and placed my hand over his heart.

He gave me a slow smile, his eyes twinkling with a hint of mischief. "Is that so?"

"Yes." I grabbed his hand and pulled him toward the bed, ready to show him the same care he'd shown me in the shower. It was remarkable how being pampered by the person I loved the most had filled my heart and all the empty recesses of my soul. This was what it felt like to be loved, and I wanted to return the favor. I pulled the covers down and climbed into the bed, gesturing for him to join me.

Once we were under the covers, Jax lay on his back and tugged me to his chest. His arms went around me as he kissed me on the top of my head just like he did every night when we were ready for sleep.

I glanced up at him. "Are you tired?"

"No."

"Good. Me neither." I swung one leg over him and moved to straddle his waist. With my hands on his chest, I lowered myself until our lips were just an inch apart and whispered, "Let me love you, Jax."

His eyes searched mine for just a moment as if he was making sure this was what I really wanted. Whatever he saw there must have satisfied him because his eyes heated and his tongue darted out, licking his lips before he nodded once.

Trailing my fingers over his chest, I dipped my head and pressed light, open-mouth kisses on his neck.

Jax's body jerked slightly with a tiny shiver that made me smile. If there was one thing that drove him crazy, it was when I took my time exploring him. That fire that burned hot between us always sent us both into a needy desperation. Drawing that out, making him wait, was a sweet, lovely torture. But this wasn't just about sex. It was about showing him how much I loved him. When I moved lower and bit down lightly where his shoulder met the base of his neck, his hands tightened on my hips.

"Marion," he murmured. "Damn, I love it when you do that."

I smiled against his skin and bit him gently again, pleased when I felt his cock twitch against my belly.

"If you keep that up, I'm liable to lose control."

"No, you aren't," I said softly. "I know you better than that."

He let out a husky chuckle. "You do realize that touching you like that in the shower was a slow torture, right?"

I just gave him a slight shrug. I hadn't actually thought of that, though I should have. He'd touched every inch of my body. The body that he worshipped almost every night. "I'm certain you're up for the challenge."

His eyes closed as I moved down his body, one hand skimming down his side as the other found his right nipple. Just as I wrapped my lips around the left one, I pinched the right one gently.

"Fuck," Jax said with a groan. "Marion, goddamn."

I took my time worshipping his defined pecs and teasing his nipples until his breathing became labored. One of his hands was buried in my hair, holding me in place, and the other was clasped over my bare ass, squeezing so hard I wouldn't have been surprised if there was a mark there in the morning.

Glancing down, I spotted the wetness at the tip of his cock and smiled to myself before moving lower, dropping kisses over his taught abs. When my mouth hovered just over his pulsating dick, he stared down at me with so much heat I thought I might combust right then and there.

Holding his gaze, I licked at his salty tip, drawing it out as he nearly growled his frustration.

"What do you want, Jax?" I asked, barely recognizing my own husky voice.

"You know what I want, baby," he said, his hips jerking up slightly.

"Yeah, I do." Placing my hand around the base of his shaft, I dipped my head and wrapped my lips around him.

"Yes," he hissed, his hips pulsating up and down in tiny movements so that he didn't choke me.

I kissed, sucked, and tasted, giving him everything I had until he pulled me off him and turned us so quickly that I let out a small gasp of surprise.

"That's enough," he said and crushed his lips to mine, claiming me.

I let myself get lost in his kiss, my head swimming in pure desire as he slowly entered me. My back arched and I tilted my hips to meet him halfway, reveling in the sensation of having him fill me, of his weight pressing me into the bed, of the taste of his tongue on mine.

Our lovemaking was slow and deliberate. Both of us holding back, taking our time to appreciate the moment. Drawing it out in a slow, sweet torture that made my entire body tremble with need.

Finally, I'd had enough. My hands moved to grab his ass, and I said, "Make me come, Jax."

He let out a low growl and unleashed himself, thrusting into me over and over and over again, until he finally shifted, hitting the exact right spot that made my body stiffen and my toes curl. We both cried out together, clinging to each other as we rode out one of the most intense orgasms I'd ever had.

When the tidal wave passed, Jax stared down at me, his eyes full of tenderness. "I wasn't expecting that tonight."

"I know," I answered and wrapped my arms around him, pulling him down so that his full weight was resting on me. "I just needed you."

He gave me a whisper of a kiss as he brushed my still wet hair out of my eyes. Then he smiled. "It's good to be needed."

Chuckling, I gently pushed him off me and then rolled into his arms, resting my head on his chest.

We were silent in the darkness until he finally said, "Do you want to talk about today?"

I closed my eyes and sucked in a deep breath. "Can it wait until morning?"

He nodded and then held me as I drifted off into a restless sleep.

CHAPTER 8

"*W*ake up, sunshine," Jax said.

I blinked up at him, the sun making me wince. There was a dull ache over my left eye, and my body was heavy with sleep. Scowling, I peered up at him. "Why? Just why?"

Without a word, he handed me a mug of coffee.

I sat up and pressed a hand to my head, trying to dull the pain. What the hell was that about? It's not like I'd been drinking the night before.

"Goddess-summoning headache?" he asked.

"How did you know?" We hadn't talked about my day the night before. We'd just fallen into each other's arms. One would think after a night of pampering and an intense orgasm that I'd have woken up with a pep in my step instead of feeling like I'd gotten into a brawl and lost. I took a sip of the coffee and let out a sigh of pleasure.

"Ty mentioned it." He sat down on the edge of the bed

and placed a light hand on my knee. "They're all worried about you."

I closed my eyes and leaned against the headboard. Of course they were. I would be worried too if any of them were in a situation like mine. "I'm fine."

"Are you?" There was concern in his dark eyes.

"As fine as I can be, I suppose." I took another sip of the coffee, grateful for his thoughtfulness. "I'm sorry our trip was ruined."

"You don't have anything to be sorry about." He cupped my cheek with his palm and leaned in to give me a lingering kiss. "It's just a trip up the coast. Nothing we can't reschedule."

"I know, but—"

He placed his fingers over my lips, quieting me. "You couldn't control this anymore than I could've controlled the vandalism at my construction site earlier this year. We'll take the trip once we're past this."

He was right. Why did I feel so guilty about this? It wasn't my fault any of this had happened. At least I didn't think it was. My mind started to race with a million unanswered questions, and despite my aching head and limbs that felt like they'd been covered in quicksand, I pulled the covers back and climbed out of bed.

There were things to do and people to call. After a quick shower, I brushed my teeth and pulled on my favorite pair of ripped jeans and a T-shirt. Thankfully, the shower along with the caffeine had started to ease my headache, and despite the daunting task of trying to navigate the latest disaster, I was feeling stronger and ready to tackle whatever the day threw at us.

As I headed for the door, Jax said, "Marion?"

"Yeah?" I answered, smiling at him. But when I saw the concerned expression on his face, I felt that ache of unease settle in my gut again. "What happened?"

"It's Ty. He has a visitor and you're going to want to meet him."

I frowned. "He does? Who?"

"His name is Carson…" Jax took a deep breath and said, "He claims to be Ty's brother."

I stood stock-still for a long moment, trying to make sense of what Jax had just said. But the sentence didn't compute. "That's impossible," I finally said. "Trish didn't have any other children."

Jax raised his hands, palms up. "He has a birth certificate that says otherwise."

My heart started to race as my adrenaline kicked in. "Impossible." But before Jax could say another word, I hurried out of my room and followed the muted voices into the kitchen.

Ty's head jerked up as soon as he heard my footsteps. His face was pale, and he looked like he'd been gut-punched.

Immediately, my mama-bear instincts kicked in and I went to stand beside him, placing one hand on his shoulder.

The man who was sitting across from him was a few years older than Ty with the same curly dark hair and dark eyes. Carson was a slightly larger-framed version of Ty. Even without looking at a birth certificate, it would be hard to deny that they were related.

Carson stood, revealing he was a couple of inches taller than Ty, and held out his hand. "You must be Marion."

With my heart caught in my throat, I held my hand out

to the younger man. How old was he? Late twenties? Early thirties? It was hard to tell. "And you are?" I asked, even though I already knew his name.

He cleared his throat. "Carson Kirkwood."

"Kirkwood?" I asked, unable to stop myself. That was Trish's last name. The one she'd given Ty when his father walked out before Ty was born.

His cheeks tinged pink as he dropped my hand and shoved his into his pockets. "Yeah. I suppose that comes as quite the shock."

"A little bit." A whole hell of a lot, actually.

Ty cleared his throat and pointed at a piece of paper sitting on the table. "According to this, Carson was born while Mom was in college."

I glanced at the birth certificate and zeroed in on the date. Sure enough, Carson's birthday was when Trish would've been a junior in college at a school across the country from me. He was born in late April. After some quick math, I came to the conclusion that the father likely was from our hometown and not someone she met at college. My gaze moved up to the parents. Trish Kirkwood was listed as his mother. But just like Ty's birth certificate, the father was listed as unknown.

Either Carson was a skilled conman, or this was legit. The birth certificate, along with his physical appearance, was just too convincing. I turned to look at Ty. The raw expression on his face told me he was gutted and that he too believed that he was sitting across from his biological half brother.

My head started to pound again.

"I know this is a shock," Carson said. "You have no idea

how long I've been trying to talk myself into coming up here to meet Ty."

"What made you decide now was the right time?" I asked, wincing when my tone sounded accusatory. If this man really was Trish's son, then he deserved this meeting. And he deserved for me to treat him with respect. "I'm sorry. It's just been... a rough couple of days already, and this news... Well, as you said, it's a huge shock."

"I understand completely," he said. "But to answer your question, the reason I'm here today is because I've been offered a job here in Premonition Pointe, and I'm moving here. I just couldn't imagine living in this town, knowing I have a brother, and not meeting him."

"A job?" I asked, my eyebrows shooting up. "Where?"

"Sky's the Limit. It's a—"

"It's a store owned by my friend Skyler," I said. "He's a designer."

"That's right." The man smiled. "I'm a junior designer. He's bringing me on as an apprentice."

I shared a look with Ty.

"What?" Carson asked.

Ty ran a hand through his dark hair. "Nothing. It's just... Kennedy works at Sky's the Limit, too."

"Kennedy?" Carson asked. "Should I know who that is?"

Ty's fist tightened, and I recognized it as a stress response. Was he worried about what his brother would say or think when he found out Ty was in a same-sex relationship? Once Ty had come out to me, he hadn't been one to shy away from his truth with anyone else. But coming out to a brother he'd just met might be more intimidating.

"Kennedy is my boyfriend," Ty said, staring the other man dead in the eye as if almost daring him to make something of it.

"Oh." Carson glanced away quickly before meeting Ty's gaze again with a small smile. "That's cool."

Ty blinked. "It is?"

"Yeah." Carson let out a small chuckle. "I'm bi. I actually got the job at Sky's the Limit through my ex-boyfriend. He does modeling for Skyler."

Ty's entire body seemed to relax all at once. "Really? Your ex hooked you up with a job?"

Carson's grin turned lopsided. "Sort-of ex. We still…" He glanced at me, his cheeks reddening again. "Let's just say we're still friends."

I couldn't help it. I laughed.

Ty laughed too, and suddenly all the tension between the two men disappeared. "Don't worry about Marion, Carson," Ty said, his eyes twinkling with amusement. "Before Jax entered the picture, all of her relationships could have been classified as friends with benefits."

"Hey!" I cried, half offended, half amused. "That's not fair. I dated."

Ty raised one mocking eyebrow. "Dated? No. You did hookups."

"The matchmaker didn't date?" Carson asked, his expression matching Ty's amused one.

"Nope. She wasn't interested in anything long-term," Ty confirmed.

"That's because she was waiting for me," Jax said, entering the kitchen. He walked over to the counter and poured himself another cup of coffee. "She met me in high school, and I guess I ruined her for everyone else." He winked at me. "It only took her thirty years to come to her senses after she dumped me."

"Oh my gods!" I threw my hands up. "It's nice that you all are bonding over my choice not to settle down when I was younger, but can we move on now?"

Ty wrapped one arm around my shoulders and pulled me in for a sideways hug. "Don't be upset, Marion. I just wanted Carson to know that you aren't some uptight traditionalist who thinks everyone should settle down into marriage or something. I wasn't slut-shaming you."

"Me neither," Jax said right before taking a sip of coffee. "I was bragging about the fact that I finally landed the free spirit of my dreams."

I rolled my eyes. "Nice save."

Carson chuckled and sat back in his chair, looking relieved. "I have to tell you; I was really nervous coming here. But you guys… Well, you're all great."

Ty reached across the table and squeezed Carson's hand. "Even though this is a huge shock, I'm glad you're here. Do you maybe want to take a walk? I'd really like to learn more about you."

"I'd like that very much." Carson stood, and the pair of them headed out of the house.

I stared after them, so many questions on the tip of my tongue. The important ones that I'd been too stunned to voice. I wanted to call for them to come back so I could make some sense of what had happened all those years ago. Where had Carson been? Were he and Trish in touch? How had he found out about Ty? Did he have any idea who his father was? But most of all, I wanted to know why Trish hadn't told me about him.

My heart ached for my friend who'd gone through a pregnancy on her own and hadn't thought she could tell me. I also felt betrayed. Why hadn't she trusted me? I'd have been there for her without judgment. She hadn't needed to keep that kind of secret to herself. Had she given him up for adoption? I supposed she must have. What a heart-wrenching decision that must have been.

I stared down at the birth certificate Carson had left on the table, willing it to give me some clue to the past. But there was nothing beyond a birthdate and Trish's name.

"Marion?" Jax asked, coming to stand beside me. "Are you okay?"

"No." I shook my head. "Not okay at all." I closed my eyes, squeezing them tight, and did my best to swallow the scream that was building in my chest.

He sat down and placed his hand over mine, just holding it, letting me work through my emotions on my own.

When I finally opened my eyes, I said, "Something isn't right."

"What isn't?" he asked.

"Carson. He might be Trish's son, but him showing up right after the social media blow-up and someone hacking into my computer... Don't you think it's suspicious?"

"It could be. Or it could just be a coincidence."

"No." I shook my head, certain in my gut that I wasn't wrong. "He's bad news, Jax. I know it."

CHAPTER 9

*T*y and Carson were gone for over an hour, and I was starting to pace.

"Would you relax?" Charlotte said from her spot where she was curled up at the end of the couch, painting her nails.

"I can't. Not until I find out why Carson is really here." I crossed the living room and peered out the front window.

"You do realize that he's probably just here to meet his brother, right?" Charlotte screwed the cap back on the nail polish bottle. "Not everyone who shows up in Premonition Pointe is here to cause trouble."

I just stared at my sister.

"What?" Her eyes were wide with innocence. "I'm not wrong."

I huffed out a laugh. "Just like when you showed up. Didn't you roll into town with a curse that was clinging to you?"

"So?" she said defiantly. "It's not like I was *trying* to hurt anyone."

She had a point. The real reason she'd come to town was because she needed help and didn't have anywhere else to go. She hadn't intended to cause trouble for anyone.

"That's true," I conceded. "But we know nothing about this man. We don't know how long he's known about Ty or why he showed up today of all days. I have a right to be suspicious."

"So be suspicious. Just stop pacing. You're giving me motion sickness."

"No, I'm not," I said, unable to hide my exasperation.

"Okay, you're just getting on my last nerve," she said. "What do you have to say about that?"

I opened my mouth to respond but was cut off when my phone rang. I quickly grabbed it, and when I saw Sebastian's name flash across the screen, I accepted the call. "Have you found anything?"

"I'm still waiting for results from the fingerprint sweep at your office," Sebastian said. "And my tech guy is still running traces on your computer to see what was accessed."

"Okay." I walked out onto the front porch and sat in my wooden swing. "So, is this just an I'm-still-working-on-it call?"

"Yes and no." He paused and I heard an audible gulp as if he'd just taken a drink of something. "That's where we're at with the investigation at your office. But I've also taken on Sara Groveland as a client. She's been released from the police department as of this morning, and I was hoping that you'd grant me permission to look at all of the files of the men you set her up with."

"Of course. If it helps with the case," I said automatically.

"Since you've agreed to be her lawyer, I assume that means you think she's innocent."

"I don't know exactly what to think to be honest with you. But I do think it's unlikely that Sara poisoned all of her dates. The fact that she was arrested the same day that your office was targeted is setting off all my alarm bells."

I nodded my agreement, even though he couldn't see me. "If you think that's bad, I have another one for you."

"You can't be serious."

"Oh, I'm deadly serious." I quickly filled him in on our morning visitor and ended with, "He seems legit, but I can't shake the feeling that he's somehow connected to the break-in and maybe even Sara's case. It's just too much of a coincidence for this all to happen at the same time."

"You think Ty's brother had something to do with the poisonings?" Sebastian sounded dubious.

"I know it sounds crazy. Maybe I'm just paranoid."

"Let's just see how everything plays out. What does Carson want? Has he asked Ty for anything?"

"No," I said. "At least not that I know of. He said he's been wanting to meet Ty and now that he has a job here with Skyler, he decided it was time. Though I'm not sure how he even found out about Ty in the first place."

"That sounds legit enough. Do you want me to do a background check on him?"

Everything inside of me screamed yes. But a voice in the back of my head warned me that might not be the best idea. At least not until I talked to Ty about it. "No. Not yet. Let me talk to Ty. I think I might have just been thrown for a loop. It's hard to fathom Trish not telling me about him."

"I imagine it was a huge shock. I'm sure your friend had her reasons."

"She must have," I reluctantly agreed. Trish and I had been as close as sisters. While I hadn't been at the hospital when Ty was born, I had been there right after. How had I not known she'd had a child before? Was that why Ty had come so quickly? Trish had gone into labor, and by the time she made it to the hospital, Ty was already making an appearance.

I recalled overhearing the nurses talking about how it wasn't unusual for labor to be quick with second babies. I'd just assumed they were talking about someone else. But now? Obviously, I'd been the one in the dark.

"I'll get those files to you. They're on my laptop, too, so I'll send them over this morning," I told Sebastian. "That way you won't have to go digging around in the computer your tech is still analyzing."

"I appreciate it, Marion. When the prints come back and I hear from my tech, I'll give you a call."

Right as I ended the call, Jax and Minx strolled up the walkway and onto the porch. He'd taken the chihuahua on a walk around the neighborhood.

"Are you okay?" Jax asked me.

"Sure. Why? Do I look stressed or something?"

"A little," he said and then gave me a kiss on the cheek as I stood.

"I just spoke to Sebastian. He's going to represent Sara."

"That's a good thing, right?"

I nodded. "I'm just still freaked out about Carson showing up here in the midst of all this. My track record of people just showing up out of the blue is pretty dubious. No one seems to come to town unless trouble is following them."

"I can't deny that's true, but it can't be one hundred percent of the time, can it?"

"I don't know."

"Let's just try to see where this goes before we jump to conclusions. Ty deserves that much, right?"

I reluctantly agreed and followed them back inside the house.

"That's a good girl, Minx," he said as he scratched her ears before freeing her from her harness. The little dog swiped her tongue up his cheek and then spun around in circles, desperate for her after-walk treat.

"You spoil her," Charlotte said, shaking her head.

"It's what she deserves," he said, snatching Minx into his arms to take her to the kitchen.

"That's either really sweet or really disturbing," Charlotte said as she watched them go.

I chuckled. "It's sweet. And way better than Minx trying to bite his junk off the way she did when they first met."

"True." Charlotte inspected her freshly painted nails. "And I certainly don't mind that he likes to take her on walks. Especially when it's overcast and cold out. Jax makes an exceptional doggie daddy."

He did. There was no doubt about that. When he walked back in with Minx still in his arms, I smiled at him. "Want to take a ride with me?"

He gave Minx a kiss on the top of her head and put her on the couch next to Charlotte. "Sure. Where are we headed?"

"Groveland Farms."

CHAPTER 10

$\mathcal{J}$ ax parked his truck in the small parking lot of the farm that was a few miles inland from downtown Premonition Pointe. There was a quaint cottage that had been turned into a small store and behind it, there was a large lavender field and two more plots that were filled with a variety of vegetables.

"It looks pretty quiet," Jax said. "Do you think Sara is even here?"

I walked over to the store and tried the door. Locked. After peering in a window and noting there weren't any lights on, I said, "If she is, she must be out back somewhere." I glanced at my phone where I'd logged her address. "She gave me this street number for her home address. Do you see a house anywhere, besides the store?"

"No. But there's a road right there that leads into those trees. Maybe that's it."

I turned and spotted the dirt road that I hadn't noticed when we'd driven up. "Looks like it's worth a shot."

Together we walked up the dirt driveway. When we'd gone about a half mile, I asked Jax, "What do you think we're going to find at the end of this road?"

"A distillery," he said.

"Moonshine?" I asked with a laugh.

"Maybe. Or a secret lab where Sara makes her poison potions and sells them on the black market."

I gave him a flat stare. "Don't even say that."

He smirked.

"Seriously, I know you're joking, but at the rate things have been going, I just wouldn't be surprised."

"Maybe it's a secret marijuana farm," he guessed.

"Now that's something that wouldn't surprise me." Even though weed was legal in California now, there were still a bunch of people who'd been growing and selling illegally for years who'd opted to forgo getting expensive licenses from the state to start selling legally. And if they had any sort of criminal background, forget it. They'd never be approved anyway.

We continued to banter about what might be hidden in the trees until we finally came upon a pretty little log cabin with a wraparound deck. Two vehicles were parked out front. I recognized Sara's red Toyota truck, but not the sleek metallic blue Lexus SUV with Oregon plates.

"She looks to have company," I said, waving at the SUV.

"Marion?" Sara's familiar voice called out.

I glanced around and spotted her standing next to a large tree off to the left of her house. Behind her was a small garden and a bench where a lean man with salt-and-pepper hair sat studying us.

"What are you doing here?" Sara asked, moving toward us.

"We just came to check on you. After your ordeal last night, I wanted to make sure you were okay," I said.

The petite brunette let out a frustrated sigh as she quickly tied her long hair into a low ponytail. "Now that I'm home and Andrew is here, I'm doing much better. Thank you for calling Sebastian for me. He was a huge help in getting me released."

"You're welcome." I glanced at the man still sitting on her garden bench, trying to place him. Was he a family member? "Is Andrew your brother?"

"What? No. I don't have a brother," she said, shaking her head. "He's a friend from my small farm group on Facebook. He's a lawyer and has experience in representing small farms in food poisoning cases. I just called Sebastian to let him know I'm going to use Andrew as my lawyer instead."

"You're changing lawyers already?" I asked, trying to keep my dismay in check. Sebastian was the best around, and maybe more importantly, he was the only lawyer I'd ever met that I trusted.

"Yes. Like I said, he has experience with this sort of thing, and because he's a friend, it's free, so it's really the best option for me." She waved at him.

The man on the bench gave her a slight nod and then continued to stare at us. The interaction didn't make me feel any better.

"I see," I said and cleared my throat, wondering just how well she knew this Andrew guy from Oregon. And how exactly had he gotten there so fast? Had the police let her have more than one phone call last night? "Free is certainly good," I hedged. "Have you known Andrew long?"

She pursed her lips in thought. "Maybe about six months? He helped another member of our group not long ago, so I feel really lucky that he came right over the moment he heard."

How had he heard? Hadn't she been in jail until that morning? "Over from where?" I couldn't help asking. "Oregon?"

"Oh no," she said, shaking her head. "He's been staying with his sister about forty miles north of here. Isn't that lucky?"

"Lucky. Sure."

The front door swung open and another man, this one short and stocky with wire-rimmed glasses, came bounding out. He had a piece of paper in his hand that he held high over his head. He hurried toward Andrew. "Results are negative!"

"Negative?" Sara cried, clutching her chest. Tears spilled from her eyes as she smiled at me. "Negative. That means none of my stock tested positive for poison."

Jax and I shared a curious glance.

"You're having your stock analyzed?" I asked her, trying to understand what was going on. "What stock?"

"My jams. Before each date you set up for me, I had a package of my jams sent as an introduction about me and what I do. The detective and his minions took all of my stock from the store to have it tested. They said that's what poisoned my dates. But I had some here at home from that same batch, and I wanted to know if there was any truth to the idea that my jams were toxic, so Andrew brought over someone to test them. He just said he didn't find anything. Isn't that great? Once the police test my jams, they'll see that they are mistaken and all of this will be over."

Somehow, I doubted that was the case. If they had enough evidence to arrest her, they weren't going to drop it when they found out the stock she was selling wasn't poisoned. Besides, what made her think they wouldn't just assume she'd poisoned the jars she'd sent to her dates? "Sara, I'm not sure—"

"Sara," Andrew called.

"Yes?" She smiled at him adoringly.

"It's better if you don't talk about the case." He stood at the edge of her small garden with his hands in his pockets.

"Right," she said and started to move toward him without even saying a word to us. When she reached his side, he clasped her hand and tugged her in close to him. With their heads bent together, they followed the shorter lab guy back into her house.

"That was strange," Jax said.

I was frozen in my spot, staring at the house, unable to process what had just gone down.

"Let's go," Jax said, clasping my hand with his.

"You don't think I should try to get more information about this Andrew guy?"

"Do you really think he's going to tell you anything?" Jax was already moving down the driveway. "He just ordered her to stop talking to you and then led her into the house. I think it's pretty clear where he stands."

I closed my eyes for a long moment, trying to collect myself. "That entire interaction was off, wasn't it? Sara didn't even say goodbye."

"She did spend the night in jail. Maybe she's just overwhelmed."

That was possible, but I still couldn't shake the feeling that this Andrew guy was suspicious.

Or was it just me?

Was I being overly protective? First I'd been suspicious of Carson and now this Andrew guy. Not everyone could be a bad actor. Right? Was I just seeing villains everywhere? Maybe all the trouble with curses both Charlotte and I had experienced over the past year had jaded me. Trust wasn't easy to come by when things were going sideways.

"I can't just leave without asking Sara some questions," I said as I came to a stop. "I at least have to try."

Jax studied me for a long moment and then nodded. "Yeah, I can see that."

After pressing up on my tiptoes to give him a kiss on the cheek, I hurried back to the cabin and knocked on the door.

"Marion?" Sara asked as she stepped out onto the porch. "I thought you and Jax had left."

"Not yet," I said cheerfully, trying to hide my annoyance.

"Well, I'm kind of busy with Andrew. If you don't mind, I really don't have time to deal with my dating life right now, so—"

"Dating life?" I asked, unable to hide the incredulity in my voice. "I'm not here to talk about that."

"Oh." She glanced back over her shoulder for a moment and then back at me. "Andrew doesn't want me talking about the case."

"I understand that, but unfortunately, I'm involved now. Did you hear about the break-in at my office?"

She gave me a solemn nod. "I don't know anything about that, though."

"I didn't figure you did. I just want to know if you have any ideas about who could have poisoned your dates. Any guesses at all? If you were investigating, where would you start?"

Sara pressed her lips together into a thin line and took a deep breath. "Honestly, Marion, I'd start with you and your staff. Your dating agency is the common denominator. And when you add in the fact that your place was targeted yesterday, I'm guessing the attacker is one of your clients."

Frustration coiled in my gut and felt like it was crawling up my throat. My initial impulse was to lash out at Sara, to remind her that she called me for help. But she had a point. The attacker appeared to be connected to my dating agency. From her perspective, she was the innocent bystander who'd been unfairly targeted.

I blew out a long breath. "You could be right. It's hard to say at this point. All I'm trying to do is figure out who did this so that we can clear your name and no one else gets hurt. I thought—"

"I'm sorry, Marion," Sara said, giving me an apologetic look. "I really can't help you. Andrew told me not to say anything to anyone while the case is still ongoing."

"About Andrew," I said, knowing that I should have just respected her wishes and left her alone, but I couldn't go without at least trying to make sure she wasn't making a huge mistake with her Facebook lawyer. "I'm sure he's great, but Sebastian is the best in the state when it comes to investigations and legal matters. I've worked with him before and honestly, there's no one I trust more."

"Well, that's good for you, Marion," she said, sounding annoyed. "I'm glad you trust your friend. I'm sure that will help you understand why I trust mine. Thank you for your help, but I'm in good hands now."

I opened my mouth to respond, but before I could get any words out, she gently shut the door. A second later, I heard the unmistakable sound of the lock sliding into place.

"Dammit," I muttered and walked back down to where Jax was waiting for me.

"Judging by the look on your face, I'm guessing that didn't go as well as you hoped," Jax said, pressing his hand to my lower back as we walked down the long driveway.

"No. It absolutely didn't." I chewed on my bottom lip and added, "In fact, it went so poorly that I'm no longer convinced Sara is innocent."

His eyes widened as he raised both eyebrows. "Really?"

I took a moment to do a quick gut check and then nodded once. "Really. That woman back there isn't the one who hired me for my matchmaking services. I don't know where that woman is or if she even ever existed."

"She can't be the one who broke into your office," Jax reasoned. "She was in police custody when that happened."

"No, but we don't know where Andrew was this morning."

"Or his little science-nerd sidekick," Jax said.

"Exactly. It looks like Sebastian is going to have to do a couple more background checks." I glanced back at the vehicle with Oregon plates and made a quick note of the license number for Sebastian. It would be a start.

84

CHAPTER 11

*W*hen we were back in Jax's truck, I pulled out my phone and called Sebastian.

"Sara fired me," he said without any greeting.

"I heard. She has some new lawyer she met on Facebook. We were just at her place and he's there now."

Sebastian groaned.

"Funny, I had the same reaction," I said. "Some guy named Andrew. Would it be a terrible breach of ethics if you ran a background check on him?"

"Probably, but that doesn't mean I won't. Do you have his last name?"

"No, but I did get the plate number off his vehicle. You could probably get his name from that, or maybe since he's her new lawyer, there's some sort of record with the court," I suggested.

"Yes. One of those will work."

I rattled off the number and then said, "Thank you. With everything going on, I'm just not sure I can trust anyone." I went on to explain my suspicion of Sara and Carson. "It's just too much all at once, and my Spidey sense is pinging off the charts."

"It does seem like an unusual coincidence that Carson showed up right after your office was targeted," Sebastian said, sounding just as skeptical as I'd felt. "Are you certain he's your friend's son?"

"No, but he did have a birth certificate. It looked real to me."

"You know those can be faked, right?"

I let out a humorless laugh. "Yes, I considered that, but wait until you see him. There's no denying he and Ty are related."

"Hmm." There was typing on the other end of the line. "Carson Kirkwood?"

"Yes, but Sebastian, I meant it when I said I don't want to run any background checks or anything until I talk to Ty. If Carson's for real, I don't want their relationship to start out on that sort of note."

"Uh-huh," he murmured. "Noted. You're only asking me to run a check on Sara's new lawyer."

I knew exactly what that meant. He was reiterating that he understood that I wasn't asking him to go digging around in Carson's past, but that didn't mean he wouldn't on his own. And honestly, I wasn't mad about it. He'd only say anything if he found something suspicious. "Correct. There's also a science guy at Sara's, running tests on her jams, but I have no idea what his name is."

"Got it. If I turn up some sort of connection in Andrew's past that matches someone who might work at a lab, I'll check him out, too. In the meantime, I'm still looking at the clients who were poisoned to see if we find any clues. Now I'm adding Sara to the list just to be thorough."

"I don't know that you'll find anything on them since we've already run a standard background check on all of them. It's company policy before I provide any matchmaking services."

"I imagine our methods are a bit more thorough than the service you contract with," Sebastian said in a matter-of-fact tone.

"Okay then," I said with a sardonic chuckle. "In the meantime, I think I'm going to search each of those guys out and get their side of the story. See if I can turn anything up."

There was silence on the other end of the line.

"Sebastian?"

"I'm here. I'm just trying to determine whether that's a good idea or not. Legally you could be opening yourself up to a lawsuit if you say the wrong thing. But more importantly, if these guys were targeted, who's to say they won't be targeted again? It would be much safer for you personally if you stayed away from them."

"Since when have I ever played anything safe when it comes to protecting my business and my family?" I asked, thinking about how Ty might now be caught up in this and how sick Charlotte had gotten off the energy left behind in my office.

"I thought you'd say that," he said with a soft chuckle. "They do need to be interviewed, and it's likely they'll be more willing to talk to you since they know you. Just do me a favor and take Charlotte with you. If you're attacked, the two of you together seem to be able to handle just about anything."

"I will," I promised. "And then I'll report back anything we find."

"I'll do the same after we get through the data analysis and background checks." He paused for a moment. "Marion?"

"Yeah?"

"Be careful. Gigi will have my head if anything happens to you while you're out sleuthing."

I couldn't help the small smile that tugged at my lips. "Don't worry. I'll keep you out of hot water with Gigi and the rest of the coven." They knew me well enough by now to know I was the *jump in with both feet and deal with the consequences later* type of gal.

As I ended the call, Jax glanced over at me. "I want to go with you and Charlotte to interview those guys."

I raised my eyebrows. "You're not afraid that Charlotte and I can't handle ourselves, are you?"

He scoffed. "No. But if I was, I certainly wouldn't touch that question with a ten-foot pole."

"Then why now?" I asked curiously. Jax didn't usually go with me when I was investigating anything paranormal. He didn't have any magical abilities, so it wasn't exactly his field of expertise.

"Since we were supposed to be up north this week, I've already taken the time off. I'd rather spend that time with you instead of sitting at home, worrying about how your day has gone." He lifted one arm and flexed, showing off an impressive bicep. "Besides, I figure it wouldn't hurt to take some muscle along… just in case."

I laughed, grateful for the levity. It had been a long two days. "You know what? I think I'd love that."

"Excellent. It's a plan."

"I CAN'T BELIEVE you set Sara up with such dweebs," Charlotte said with a look of horror. "I mean, there is just nothing sexy at all about a man named Norman Netterbaum."

"Norman Netterbaum?" Jax asked, his eyebrows raised to his hairline. "That's a guy you call when you need a root canal. Not one who makes a woman's toes curl."

"Actually, he runs a farm-to-table co-op, and he's the guy you call when you have questions about organic fertilizers," I said with a sniff.

They both stared at me like I had two heads.

"What? Sara runs a farm. On paper, they had a lot in common." The three of us were sitting at my dining room table, going over the files of the five men I'd matched with Sara so we could make a plan to start interviewing them.

"What about their auras?" Charlotte asked.

"They were a match," I said, aware my tone was defensive now. "As you well know." Ever since I'd been cursed not long after I'd moved to Premonition Pointe, I could only see auras when Charlotte and I were connected. "You were there when I made the list of contenders for Sara. I don't know why you're so shocked now."

"First of all, if I'd known his name was Norman, I'd have put the kibosh on that, post haste. Second, you know I don't pay that much attention to the actual details. There's only one thing I worry about; making sure their auras show at least a hint of passion." Charlotte narrowed her eyes at me. "Were there any tinges of red at all when they were near each other?"

"Well, no, but—"

My sister put her hand up, stopping me. "I rest my case. How many times do I need to tell you that without that red hue in their auras, you're doing them a disservice?"

I sucked in a long breath. "That's not how it works, Charlotte," I said for the hundredth time. My gift had always been that I could see auras and know when two people were perfect for each other. Red signified passion, but it wasn't the most important color. And it certainly wasn't necessary. I'd matched dozens of couples who'd never shown that red color in their auras and were still going strong ten to twenty years later.

"I know, I know. Purple is the holy grail in aura matching," she said, rolling her eyes. "Whatever. Give me that fiery-hot red aura any day over stable and boring. Just like you and Jax."

"You and Denver have fuchsia auras when you're together," I said, feeling smug. Denver was her boyfriend, and even though she often acted like their relationship was just casual, I knew better. He was her long game. She just needed time to get used to the idea.

"That's because the red is mixing with the purple to make it that color. Trust me, there's plenty of passion there." She blew on her nails and pretended to buff them on her shirt.

"Red and purple makes magenta, not fuchsia," I said as if that was a sound argument.

My sister gave me a flat stare. "Seriously? That's the hill you want to die on?"

She might have had a point, but I'd be damned if I'd give her the satisfaction of knowing she was right. Besides, all that mattered was that she was happy with Denver. "I'm happy for you," I said, smiling softly at her.

"Stop looking at me like that."

"Like what?"

"Like you're getting ready to pick out your bridesmaid dress. Cool your tits, will you? Denver and I... We're still figuring stuff out."

I held my hands up in a surrender motion. "I didn't say anything about a wedding."

"No, but you were thinking it," she muttered and wrote down another name. "This guy isn't any better. What does Frank Filapot do for a living? Clean bedpans?"

Jax snorted.

I turned and shook my head at him. "Stop encouraging her."

"What does he do?" Jax asked.

I sighed. "It doesn't really matter, does it? Let's just say he works for the city."

"Oh. Em. Gee. He's a sanitation worker, isn't he?" Charlotte asked, her eyes lit with amusement.

"No!" I crossed my arms over my chest and raised my chin. "He's an environmental engineer."

Jax let out a bark of laughter. "You set Sara up with Frankie, the guy who issues permits for septic tanks?"

"Well, that figures," Charlotte grumbled and went back to studying her nails. "Marion, I swear, it's a miracle you're still in business at all. I just can't imagine Frankie the septic guy is swoonworthy enough, even for a farm girl like Sara."

"Oh, stop it. Everyone deserves love," I insisted. "Would you rather I set her up with the surfer? Or the chef who is so full of himself that he literally refers to himself in the third person?"

A shudder ran through Charlotte's body. "A surfer would be cool as long as it isn't that guy who's always saying *'Duuuuude'* and flipping his hair over his shoulder."

"That was the one," I said, feeling justified in my righteousness. "Besides, I didn't see you coming up with any better options."

"Hmm, let's see." Charlotte tapped a finger to her lips as she considered her reply. "We should recruit the guy who owns the custom motorcycle shop and the one who runs the outdoor clothing and supply company. Oh, how about the one who owns the river rafting and snowshoeing business?"

"The river rafting guy has a long-term girlfriend, and the one who owns the custom motorcycle shop is gay. Got any other ideas?" I shot back.

"That still leaves the outdoor fitness guy. We should put him on the list," Charlotte said with a nod.

Jax cleared his throat. "As fascinating as this all is, how does recruiting fresh dating prospects help solve the current problem?"

"It's a service I feel I must provide for future clients," Charlotte said with a sniff. "But I get your point." She glanced at me. "Just write down the other three men we need to interrogate, and I'll put together a plan for us to go see them tomorrow."

"You'll put together the plan?" I asked incredulously. I loved my sister, and when push came to shove, she was a kick-ass partner in the magic department. But investigating wasn't really her thing.

"Sure. I'll set up appointments with them and everything. I've got this, Marion. You'll see."

Jax and I exchanged a glance. It was obvious neither of us shared her confidence.

"Oh, come on," she cried, throwing her hands up. "If there is one thing I'm good at, it's charming men. Right, Marion?" she asked me pointedly.

I nodded reluctantly, feeling as if she'd trapped me into agreeing to let her handle things. Giving up control wasn't exactly my strong suit.

"Good. It's settled. I'll make some phone calls and let you know when we're leaving in the morning." Charlotte stood, grabbed her laptop, and after calling for Minx to follow her, she took off for her bedroom.

"Now what?" Jax asked.

I shrugged. "I guess we can get an early start on dinner." I wasn't the best cook that ever lived, but if I didn't keep my hands busy, I was going to lose my mind waiting for Ty to come home.

We'd just made our way into the kitchen when the front door burst open.

"Marion?" Kennedy called, his voice full of urgency.

I darted out of the kitchen back into the living room. "What is it?"

"It's Ty. He needs you."

Jax appeared beside me, his hand clutching mine for support.

"Where is he?" I asked.

"In our apartment. Can you come—"

"Yes," I said, cutting him off as I pulled out of Jax's grip, already heading for the door. I glanced back at Jax. "Wait for me here?"

"Always."

I nodded at Kennedy. "Let's go."

CHAPTER 12

"What's wrong?" I asked Kennedy as we hurried to the apartment over my garage. "Is it Carson? What did he do?"

Kennedy shook his head. "I don't know. Ty won't say. He just walked into the apartment and went straight into our bedroom. He's been sitting by the window with his head in his hands, not saying a word. It's almost like he's catatonic."

Kennedy's words stopped me in my tracks. I'd only seen Ty like that once before. It was right after we'd lost Trish. He'd barely spoken for weeks after her death.

"Marion?" Kennedy moved to stand next to me. He raised his eyebrows and asked, "Are *you* all right?"

"Yes. Of course," I said quickly, squeezing his hand. "It's been a hell of a couple of days already, and it looks like it's not going to get easier anytime soon. Come on. Let's go see what we can do for Ty."

He tightened his grip around my fingers. His face was drawn, and his eyes were wide with fear. I knew then that

95

he wasn't just worried about Ty. He was terrified, and there was absolutely no time for me to have a freak-out moment.

"It's going to be okay, Kennedy," I said. "Ty got a huge shock today. I'm sure he's just processing."

"I hope that's all it is." He dropped my hand as he took the stairs two at a time, obviously in a hurry to get back into the apartment.

By the time I reached the landing, Kennedy already had the door open and their miniature Yorkie, Paris Francine, was running around in circles, barking her little head off.

"Relax, sweet pea," I soothed as I picked her up and carried her inside. "No need for the theatrics. It's just me."

The little dog licked my neck and then wiggled her tiny body with such gusto that she nearly popped right out of my hands.

"Whoa," I said, barely getting her to the ground before she did a header onto the old hardwood. "Chill out, girlfriend. You're gonna hurt yourself."

"She's a daredevil," Kennedy said, his eyes already darting toward the bedroom.

"I've got this." I scratched the pup's ear and then went and knocked on the door.

No answer.

"Ty, it's me, Mama Marion. Can I come in?"

There was a muffled, unintelligible grunt on the other side of the door.

"I'm not sure if that was an answer," I said in a teasing voice. "Mind trying again?"

There was silence again, but then I heard the unmistakable sound of footsteps on the hardwood floor. A few seconds later, Ty opened the door. He remained silent as he crossed the room to sit at the small writing desk that was under the window.

"Thank you," I said as I stepped in and closed the door behind me. Maybe if we had some privacy, Ty would be more open to talking to me. "Mind if I stay for a bit?"

Ty glanced over at me, his expression resigned. "If I told you I wanted to be alone, would you actually leave?"

"No," I said. "Not when you're like this."

"Like what exactly?" he asked, running a hand through his dark curls. "In a state of shock? Like someone who needs time to process? Or just a guy who needs to recover from feeling like I was gut-punched today?"

I made my way to his side and placed a hand on his shoulder. "None of that sounds unreasonable, but you have to know that by going silent you're scaring Kennedy, right?"

He gritted his teeth and stared at the desk as if he couldn't bear to look at me. "I guess I scared you, too, huh?"

"A little," I admitted. "Today has been a lot. I just want to make sure you're okay."

"I'm not," he admitted. "How could I have a brother and not know it? How could Mom have kept this from me?" He spit the words out, not bothering to even try to hide his anger. "She knew where he was. Did you know that?" His piercing gaze was full of suspicion.

"No," I said, shaking my head firmly. "I didn't know about Carson at all. I'm just as shocked as you are."

"Really? Are you sure about that?" He tilted his head, really studying me. His tone was flat, void of emotion when he spoke again. "If you were me, would you believe she never told her best friend that she gave a baby up for adoption?"

It was my turn to raise my eyebrows as I slowly sat on the ottoman at the end of his bed. "You think I'm lying to you?"

"I honestly don't know what to think, Marion," he said with a heavy sigh. "My world was turned upside down today, and I feel like the only person I can trust is my brother, who I just met like five minutes ago."

Alarm bells started going off in my head. He trusted Carson, but not me? "Ty—"

"I'm sorry," he said with a quick shake of his head, cutting me off. "I didn't mean that. I just... It's too hard to wrap my head around the fact that Mom kept Carson a secret from everyone for nearly thirty years. Are you telling me the truth? You really didn't know?"

"I promise you; I had no idea you had a brother. Trish never said a word. I'm just as shocked as you are. In fact, I have about a million and one questions about him."

"That makes two of us," he said, distractedly tracing an old water stain on the desk with his finger.

"Do you mind sharing what you learned?" I asked. "You're not the only one reeling from today's news." I gave him a sad smile.

He shrugged. "Not much. They weren't in contact, though Mom knew where he was. She sent him a card every year for his birthday. When it didn't come the year she died, that's when he started looking for her. But instead of her, he found me. It's taken him this long to get up the nerve to introduce himself."

My heart broke for my deceased friend. A card once a year? It must have been torture for her to know exactly where her eldest son was but to never have a real relationship with him. "Where has he been all these years?"

"Up north for most of his life. On a farm in Fortuna. He was adopted by a couple, but his mom passed away when he was little. He thinks he was three. He barely remembers her. His adoptive dad raised him. It was just the two of them until his dad sold the farm and moved into an RV to travel the country." Ty let out a bark of laughter. "He wanted Carson to go with him, but Carson opted to follow his dreams instead."

"To be a fashion designer?" I asked.

Ty nodded. "He's been in the LA area for the past three years. He said it was by sheer luck that he found us here in Premonition Pointe. Something about seeing you on the news after that restaurant fire a while back."

"How did he know who I was?" It wasn't like Trish and I were related. If he'd been tracing his adoption, I shouldn't have shown up on anything. How could I? I wasn't his parent or even his godparent. I hadn't even known he existed.

"Mom told him about you. She told him if he ever needed anything and she wasn't around that he should find you. I guess she gave him your old address in LA. That's how he found me. But by the time he got the courage to contact us, we'd already moved."

"So the news brought him here," I said absently. "That was a while ago, wasn't it?"

The fire at that restaurant had been before Jax and I had even officially started dating. Carson sure took his sweet time to build up the nerve to meet us. "You don't think it's a little suspicious that Carson just showed up today? What are the odds that my office gets vandalized and then suddenly, here he is?"

Ty narrowed his eyes at me. "Why are you doing this?"

"Doing what exactly?" I asked, annoyed now. I understood that Ty's world had been knocked off its axis, but I wasn't exactly driving in a straight line at the moment either. Trish had another son. One she'd never said a word about.

"Questioning everything Carson said." He stood and placed his hands on his hips as he stared me down. "You're suspicious of him. Do you have any idea how much courage it took for him to show up here? To introduce himself to me and to you? Don't go ruining this for me or him, okay? I know things are shitty with your business, but I just don't see how you can suspect that Carson is involved."

"I'm not... okay, I *am* suspicious," I admitted as I threw my hands up. "I'm not trying to be a dick here. I'm just—"

"Used to everything going to shit," he finished for me as he moved to sit next to me on the ottoman. "I get it. I promise I do. But Carson... I really do think he's just here to get some answers and maybe some closure of his own."

"But we don't *have* any answers," I said, wondering where this version of Ty had come from. When I'd arrived at the apartment, he'd been withdrawn and seemingly unable to process what was happening. But I'd been dead wrong. Ty had been thinking about and empathizing with his brother, instead of drawing parallels and assuming that everyone was on the take somehow.

"We do have answers about some things he wants to know," Ty said. "Like what Mom was like. We also have pictures and videos of her that I'm sure Carson would like to see. She was his mother, after all, even if she did give him up and kept him a secret his entire life." Ty shook his head, clearly unable to wrap his mind around his mother's actions. "He deserves our time, however much he needs," Ty insisted.

I held back a groan but couldn't stop myself from asking, "But what if he did have something to do with the office situation? I'm not so sure we should be putting our trust in a total stranger, Ty. I'm just looking out for you."

"No, you're looking out for your business," he snapped, clearly out of patience. "He's my brother, Marion. Don't you get that?"

"Sure, I just—"

"Nope. Don't want to hear it. This is happening. I intend to have a relationship with my brother, and you can get on board or get out of the way. Those are your choices." He got up and moved to the door. Opening it, he waved, indicating my expulsion. "Goodnight, Marion."

Whoa. I'd never been dismissed so thoroughly by Ty before. There'd never been this type of coldness between us before either.

"Ty?" Kennedy said, poking his head in. His expression was no calmer than it had been earlier. "Why are you kicking Marion out?"

"I'm not kicking her out," Ty said with a roll of his eyes. "I'm just trying to end this conversation because I don't think my brother is a fraud, but she does. And I don't want to hear it."

"I never said he was a fraud," I explained as I slipped past him and headed for the front door. As I reached for the knob, I glanced back and said, "Just be careful, Ty. I worry about you."

"I'll be *fine*, Mom," he called back.

And that one word, *Mom*, was enough to settle my anxiety. It was all I needed to know that no matter how much tension was between us, Ty and I would be okay. Even if he was asking for something I couldn't give him. Because no matter how strongly Ty felt about his brother, I was certain Carson was up to something shady. It was just a feeling I had. And if there was one thing I'd learned about being a witch, it was that one should never ignore a feeling.

One way or another, I was going to find out what Carson really wanted from Ty. And I was certain it wasn't pictures or videos.

CHAPTER 13

"I thought we were going to talk to Norman," I said to my sister as we walked into Abalone, an upscale restaurant right on the beach just north of town.

"We are. Just cool your jets. Everyone has to eat." She swept in and smiled sweetly at the maître d. "Reservation for three under the name Charlotte Ray."

Jax and I shared a look of exasperation. I'd known it was a mistake to leave the planning to Charlotte. We were supposed to be getting information from the men who'd allegedly been poisoned by Sara, not lunching like we were the cast of a reality television show.

"Ah, it's lovely to see you again, Ms. Ray. Right this way. I've reserved the best table for you and your party." The tall, dark-haired man was wide shouldered and about twice as large as Jax. He looked more like a bouncer than a maître d.

"Thank you, Richard." Charlotte slipped her arm through his. She glanced up at him, smiling coyly. "You're too kind."

The man beamed down at her and guided her toward the table, never once glancing at me and Jax.

"Are you invisible?" Jax whispered in my ear.

"Now you know what it feels like to be a woman pushing fifty," I said as we moved through the sparsely populated restaurant, making me wonder where everyone was, considering it wasn't the off season yet.

He raised one eyebrow at me. "You're not serious, are you? I've seen the way men of all ages look at you. It's not subtle."

I choked out a laugh. "You must be thinking of when we were younger, because men stopped ogling me about ten years ago."

"Nope," he insisted. "Just last week, Carl over at the Bird's Eye Café was coming on to you right in front of me. I swear if you'd given him even a hint of encouragement, he'd have hauled you off to the walk-in cooler right then and there."

I scoffed. "Carl is at least seventy! And he's like that with everyone. He's just a flirt who doesn't discriminate."

"If you say so." Jax didn't seem convinced.

"Come on. You can't act like I'm supposed to be flattered that an old man is interested in me."

"What about Hollister? He's into you. He isn't seventy."

I jerked my head, staring at Jax, and promptly ran into a chair, nearly knocking me off my feet.

Jax caught me, putting me upright again. "Whoa there. Careful. You don't want to break anything, you know, in case Hollister calls and asks you to drive down to LA for a *consultation.*"

"Oh. My. Gods. Stop. There's nothing more than mutual

professional respect between me and Hollister, and you know it." Hollister Crooner was the brother-in-law of Kiera Vincent, a woman I'd help escape a terrible marriage a number of years ago. We were good friends and when she went missing not long ago, I'd worked with Hollister to bring her home.

"If you say so," Jax said with a smirk.

I honestly wanted to wipe that look right off his face. "Why are we having this conversation?"

"Because you said you feel invisible now that you're middle-aged. But I see men admiring you all the time." He shrugged one shoulder. "So maybe you just aren't paying attention."

"Apparently not as much as you are," I said dryly as I eyed him. Where had that stuff about Hollister come from? He lived miles away, and the only times we spoke these days were when we were talking about magical weapons.

"Are you two going to join me?" Charlotte called.

I glanced over where she was seated at a table right next to a floor-to-ceiling window. The view was of the Premonition Pointe bluff where the coven met regularly to cast spells and send our intentions out into the world. The sea churned just below the rocky bluff, making for a very dramatic coastline.

"Coming," I said, swatting Jax's hand away that had suddenly landed on my ass. "What was that for?" I asked, glancing over my shoulder at him.

"Just thought you could use a little nudge." There was a glint of mischief in his eyes now, telling me everything I needed to know about our previous interaction. He'd been messing with me. The Traceass.

"Are you done?" I asked Jax as I sat across from my sister.

"Nope. A man has to stay entertained somehow, doesn't he?" Jax winked at me and then picked up one of the leather-bound, oversize menus.

"Someone is feisty today," Charlotte said, an amused half smile on her face as she pumped her eyebrows at my boyfriend.

"Please stop looking at him like that," I grumbled. "He doesn't need any encouragement."

"Fine." Charlotte glanced down at her menu and pushed her lower lip out in a pout.

Jax chuckled and I ignored both of them as I looked over the menu.

Crab, shrimp, and halibut seemed to be the main draws. All of it looked good, but the prices listed made me do a double take. No wonder the place wasn't packed. Who had that kind of money for a weekday lunch? "Does that say $95 for pan seared halibut?"

Charlotte frowned at me. "Since when have you ever cared about restaurant prices?"

"Since now. What do they do, raise the fish on caviar?" With my matchmaking business temporarily closed, it wasn't like I had an income at the moment.

"Marion," Charlotte said through clenched teeth. "Now is not the time to be balking at the menu." Her eyes flickered to the left, landing briefly on the maître d as he led a very familiar man past us to his own table.

I quickly turned back to my sister and Jax. "That's Norman Netterbaum," I whispered to them both. "He's the one who left Sara sitting in the restaurant alone when he got a text from his ex-wife and left. Did you know he'd be here?"

Charlotte's lips turned upward into a self-satisfied smile. "I told you I had today handled." She winked and then got up and moved back toward the host stand, presumably looking for a restroom.

I turned to Jax. "Is my sister secretly a mastermind?"

"That remains to be seen. I'm waiting to see how she engages him before I form an opinion." Jax put his menu down just as a waiter dropped off a basket of bread. "Want a piece?" he offered as he pulled out a piece of focaccia.

"Obviously."

He chuckled and handed me the basket.

When Charlotte returned, she made a point of walking past Norman's table. Just after she passed him, something silver and shiny fell to the ground, glinting under the recessed lighting.

I opened my mouth to tell her she'd dropped something, but her pointed stare and slight shake of her head had me closing my trap immediately. *What are you up to, Charlotte?*

She was a few feet from our table when Norman suddenly called, "Excuse me, Miss. I think you've dropped this."

Charlotte paused and then turned around to face Norman. "I don't think I've— Oh! Is that my bracelet?"

Norman held up a delicate charm bracelet that was adorned with just one charm in the shape of a chihuahua. Denver had gotten it for her a couple of weeks ago, and she'd been wearing it ever since.

"You're a life saver!" Charlotte exclaimed as she ran back to him. "You have no idea how upset I'd be if I lost this." She took it and clutched the bracelet to her chest dramatically. "Thank you…" She peered at him for a long moment. "Have we met?"

The tall man with thick salt-and-pepper hair shook his head. "I don't—"

"Oh, yes. We have. You're Norman Netterbaum, aren't you?" She slipped into the chair opposite him, taking a seat at his table without an invitation.

"Yeeees," he said slowly, glancing around as if trying to figure out who'd clued her in. "How did you know that?"

"You went out on a date with one of our clients." She held her hand out to him. "I'm Charlotte Ray, sister and partner of Marion Matched of—"

"The Miss Matched Dating Agency," he said flatly. "That couldn't have been more of a mistake."

Charlotte placed an elbow on the table and then rested her chin in her hand as she leaned forward, giving him her full attention. "I heard about the poisoning. Can I just tell you that Marion and I were shocked to hear that news? I can't imagine why anyone would do such a thing."

He snorted. "No? I can. When someone's been emotionally abused the way Sara has, I suppose they think it's appropriate to punish every one of the opposite sex, no matter how kind or generous they are."

All of my warning bells went off. Emotionally abused? Where had that come from? Sara hadn't said anything about any past relationship trauma, nor had anything come up in her background check. It wasn't mandatory for a client to disclose anything that personal to me if they didn't want to, but I did encourage them to let me know if they had any triggers or hard lines that couldn't be crossed. For instance, if I knew someone had been a victim of emotional abuse before, I'd take pains to try to match them with a kind and gentle soul as opposed to someone with an alpha personality or a type-A kind of person. Intense personalities weren't always best when someone had emotional trauma they were managing. And while I was questioning things, kind and generous? Really? This was the man who up and left Sara in the middle of a date when his ex called. Unless there was an emergency, there was nothing kind about that.

I wanted desperately to ask Norman so many questions, to move to their table to be a part of the conversation, but Charlotte was handling this like a pro. I didn't want to do anything that would mess up her vibe.

"So, you really think Sara did it?" Charlotte asked, sounding horrified.

"It was her jam, and from what I heard, I wasn't the only one. Face it, Miss Ray, your client has some serious mental issues."

Clutching her chest again, Charlotte leaned forward and in a conspiratorial tone asked, "How did she do it? Lure you in with sexual favors? Make you a fancy cheesecake with jam topping and deliver it in a trench coat?"

What in the hell was Charlotte going on about? Sara had already told us she'd made gift baskets for each of them.

He let out a low chuckle. "That's some imagination you have going on in that pretty head of yours." Norman lowered his gaze, scanning her chest for a moment before meeting her eyes again. "I bet you're a fun date."

My sister preened under his admiration, flipping her long red hair back and tilting her head to the side as she let out a fake tinkling laugh. "I've never had any complaints before."

"I'm sure that's true. Why don't we get out of here? Maybe take a walk on the beach and get to know each other better?"

Okay, now this guy was just pissing me off. Did he have to be that sleazy? The only reason he'd taken such an immediate interest in Charlotte was because she brought up sexual favors and showing up in a trench coat. Could he be any more transparent? How was she sitting there smiling at him while my skin was crawling?

"Oh, you're sweet. But we haven't even had lunch yet, and I'm starved. Aren't you?" She waved a hand at his glass. "You haven't even gotten through a glass of wine yet."

"Who cares about wine when there's a gorgeous redhead flirting with them?" he asked with an exaggerated wink.

Charlotte let out a nervous chuckle, and it wasn't hard to discern that she was getting uncomfortable. The man seemed like one who wasn't going to take no for an answer, and I was starting to think that if Sara had poisoned him maybe he'd deserved it. "Well, that's very kind of you, but I hear this place has the best blackberry cobbler this side of the Rocky Mountains."

Norman's too eager grin slipped from his face and was replaced by a grimace. "I don't think I'll ever be able to eat blackberry anything ever again. Not after going to the hospital and getting my stomach pumped."

Charlotte's shoulders straightened as she sat just a little taller, obviously proud of herself. And she should be. It was impressive the way she'd steered that conversation around from his shameless flirting and right back to the night he was poisoned. "All of that over a little jam?"

"Well, jam and the fresh goat cheese that came with it," he said, his complexion turning a very pale shade of green. He pressed his hand to his abdomen and sat back in his chair, taking deep breaths. "I'll never be able to eat either one ever again."

Goat cheese? Sara didn't make any kind of cheese. She was strictly a fruit and veggie grower. In fact, if I wasn't mistaken, she might have even recently gone vegan. It seemed odd that she'd include that in a gift basket. I made a mental note to find out exactly what she'd gifted each man.

"That's unfortunate," Charlotte said, sounding sympathetic. "That combination sounds utterly delicious to me."

Norman's nose crinkled right before he stood abruptly and hurried off to the restroom.

Charlotte watched him go, and when he disappeared from view, she got up and moved back to our table. "Ready?"

I stared up at her in awe. "When exactly did you become a master at manipulating conversation?"

"Please," she said with an eye roll. "If you paid any attention to me at all, you'd know I always find a way to bring the conversation back around to whatever I want to talk about."

"True," I agreed. "But with me, you never do it that smoothly. Usually, you just cut me off and start going on about whatever's on your mind."

"Sure, with you," she said with a half shrug. "There's no

need to make you think it's your idea. I'm not trying to finesse anything. Why try?"

I let out a bark of laughter and threw some money on the table, grateful we weren't spending a hundred dollars per entrée.

Jax followed and asked, "Anyone up for Crabby's?"

"Me. I'm starved after all that." Charlotte waved at Norman's empty table. "It took more energy than you can imagine not to throw his drink in his face." Her lips curled in disgust. "Talk about a creeper."

I had to agree and wondered how he'd gotten past our screening process. No doubt he was one of those men who was skilled in normal social behavior but dropped the act the moment he thought he didn't need it anymore to impress his current conquest.

"Come on. Let's get out of here before he comes back," I said, clasping my hand around Charlotte's.

"Gladly."

Once the three of us reached my SUV, I handed Jax the keys. He took them without comment and then opened both passenger side doors for us. I nodded to the front seat, offering it to Charlotte.

"Thanks," she said and climbed in.

I took the seat behind her and leaned my head back against the leather headrest, closing my eyes and trying to process what had just happened. Had we learned anything at all of importance?

He'd said Sara was a survivor of emotional abuse.

He'd gotten sick off goat cheese, which seemed like an unusual item for Sara to include in her basket.

Anything else?

He was a creeper of the highest level who'd been ready to haul Charlotte off to the nearest broom closet to do only the goddess knew what.

"I think I need a better system for vetting eligible dates," I said.

"You got that right," Charlotte agreed.

"We'll work on it." My phone buzzed, causing me to fish it out of my pocket. "It's Sebastian," I said and answered. "What do you have for me?"

"You haven't been online today?" he asked.

My stomach roiled at his tone. "Not recently. What happened? Are there people protesting my office again?"

"Not that I'm aware of, but it's something you should be prepared for," he said, all business.

My shoulders stiffened. "Just give it to me straight, Sebastian. What should I know?"

"All right. First, I have to inform you that your client files were indeed breached. In order to stay out of hot water with the law, you'll need to contact all your clients and let them know their personal information has been compromised."

My eyes slammed closed as the reality of what he was saying hit me hard. I'd thought I was prepared for this outcome. I'd told myself that it was likely my files had been compromised. That other companies had privacy breaches and they survived, right?

"What's the second thing?" I asked, dreading the answer.

"There's been a leak to the press. Everyone already knows about the data breach. It's too late to get out in front of it. The only thing you can do is play defense now. Do you need me to write something for the press?"

"Yes," I forced out, so angry my entire body was vibrating. "I don't understand. Who leaked this? The only people who could know are your people. I haven't spoken to anyone about this other than the coven."

"The leak didn't come from us. The story broke before we even knew for sure," Sebastian explained. "My guys were still verifying."

"Which means what? Someone had a lucky guess?"

"No, Marion. It's more likely that whoever did this is the same person who leaked the story."

"But why? I just don't get it. Why are they trying to destroy my business?"

"There could be any number of reasons," Sebastian started.

The back door opened and suddenly Jax was there, sliding in next to me to wrap his arms around me. I hadn't even realized he'd stopped the vehicle.

"Gods. You two are both irritating as hell, but you're also relationship goals," Charlotte said.

I ignored my sister and sank into the warmth of Jax's arms. It wasn't that I was falling apart at the news. Not yet anyway. I'd lived through much worse. But having that extra bit of support right when I needed it was everything.

"Sebastian? Any idea on what those reasons are?" I asked as I pulled away from Jax, knowing I just needed to get through this conversation.

He sighed. "The first one that comes to mind is that someone could want revenge for the poisoning."

"That's a cheery thought. Got anything else?"

"It could be a distraction," Jax said loud enough to be heard through the phone. "If you're focused on your business, maybe you'll leave the interrogations of the alleged victims of the poisoning to someone a little less competent."

"He's right," Sebastian said. "In fact, that's probably the best explanation at this point."

"And the third reason?" I asked impatiently.

"The leaker is just a crazy person looking for attention," Sebastian said. "In all my years of doing this job, you'd be surprised at how often that seems to be the reason for taking anything to the press."

I blew out a long breath. "Okay. So what's next? Contact my clients and put out a public statement?"

"That's right," he said. "I'll send something over. Don't elaborate. Just post it online and send it to your clients. The less you say, the better off you'll be."

"Sebastian," I said, pressing my fingertips to my temple. "I can't just send an email. I work closely with my clients. They deserve a phone call."

"I really don't think—"

"Sebastian," I said, cutting him off. "I know your advice is for legal reasons, but I'm telling you that's not who I am. Work up something I can say over the phone, and I'll do my very best to stick to the script."

He didn't say anything for a long moment, but then he finally cleared his throat and said, "Okay. Just as long as you realize I'm highly against this."

"Understood."

I could practically hear Sebastian vibrating with frustration. He was a lawyer and very good at his job. He knew what he was talking about. But I just didn't run my business that way. It ran on connections and trust and open lines of communication. For me to just send an email and pretend that was fine... I just couldn't. He'd have to understand.

"I'll have something for you in the next hour," Sebastian said.

"Thanks." I ended the call and looked over at Jax. "You didn't have to stop, but thank you."

He wrapped his arm over my shoulders and kissed my head as he hugged me to him. "I'm here for whatever you need, Marion. You know that."

"Ugh, so gross," Charlotte said in an exaggerated dramatic tone. "And yet, why am I sitting here with stupid tears in my eyes? Love is disgusting."

I chuckled, grateful for her levity. "Come on." I nudged Jax. "Let's go. I have work to do."

"Office or home?" he asked as he climbed out of the back of the vehicle.

Normally, I'd have automatically said the office. I wasn't opposed to doing a little work at home, but I'd learned long ago that working from home was a balance killer. But Sebastian's team still had my work computer, and that dark energy still needed to be cleared from the office before we spent any time there. "Home. The kitchen table is about to get some use."

CHAPTER 14

"*T*his is brutal!" Charlotte announced as she threw her phone down on the table. "I can't make one more call. Not when I'm going to get my ass chewed."

"You've only made one call, and that was to Lennon Love," I said, more than frustrated with my sister. "And while she was unhappy, she hardly chewed your ass." I rolled my eyes. "She grumbled at the prospect of having to change passwords and put a lock on her credit report. She didn't threaten to sue us, or leave terrible reviews all over the internet, or even wish that you develop ass boils as penance. All of which I've endured over the last hour. But by all means, if you're done, then don't make any more calls. I'll handle it. Just like I always do."

"Well," Charlotte said slowly. "That was a bit of a rant, wasn't it?"

"Charlotte," I warned, "I'm not in the mood."

"Obviously. I'm going for a walk." She got up and strode out of the house without another word.

Jax glanced over at me. "Rough day."

"The worst," I agreed. I'd made it through three-quarters of my clients and had been yelled at, threatened, and berated enough to almost make me want to close up shop and head back to LA. But I wouldn't. I had community in Premonition Pointe. My father, aunt, sister, Jax, Ty and Kennedy, and the coven. That was way too many people to leave behind just because of a blip in my career. Though I had to admit it felt more like a giant boulder.

Still, I wouldn't give anyone the satisfaction of making me close my doors. I'd built something pretty great, and to give up now would be criminal. What was that saying? This too shall pass? I'd make damned sure of that.

"Why don't we take a break?" Jax asked, rubbing my shoulders. "Maybe head down to the coffee shop and grab a pastry or two before you finish that list."

"Thanks," I said, already shaking my head. "But I really just want to get this done and have it be over. Then I'll wallow in sugar and full-fat mochas."

He chuckled softly. "That's the Marion I know. Let me know if there's anything I can do."

I glanced at the kitchen just on the other side of the table. "You know what I'm craving?"

"Sex?" he asked, giving me an exaggerated leer.

"That would be one way to relieve all this stress," I said with a humorless laugh. "But right now, I'd kill for some shortbread cookies." Leaning forward, I gave him my best sad puppy-dog expression. "Any chance you'd mind working your magic and whipping some up for me?"

"Cookies? That's it?" he asked as he made his way to my pantry.

"For now." I gave him a secret smile, and he promptly returned it.

What I wouldn't give to just let myself get lost in Jax's arms. But I had to get through my list of clients. The sooner it was done, the sooner I could start to rebuild relationships. With a heavy sigh, I opened the next file, found the client's number, and made the next call.

Twenty minutes later, I was busy talking a different client down when a text came through. When I noticed Charlotte's name, I didn't pay it much attention. She knew what I was doing, and she'd wait a few minutes. But when a second one came in, there was no missing the multiple 911s.

"I'm so sorry, Charles," I said into the phone. "I'd be more than happy to answer all of your questions at another time, but right now there's an emergency I have to deal with."

The high-powered businessman made some remark about nothing being more important than the gross neglect we'd shown. Normally, I'd have used every ounce of charm I could muster to smooth his feathers, but today I'd just had enough. So instead of responding, I ended the call and scrolled to my texts.

They were all from Charlotte.

I might be overreacting, but there's a group of guys following me. Three of them. All three are giants, and I'm starting to feel unsafe. Can you send Jax?

Not even a minute later another text came in. *Tell him to hurry. By the Mother Stones.*

Help. 911!

"Jax!" I jumped up from the table, already moving

toward the front door. "We need to go. Charlotte's in trouble."

"What?" he called from the kitchen.

"Let's go!" I cried and jerked the closet door open next to the front door. Panicked with my heart racing, I rummaged around, tossing coats and umbrellas and reusable grocery sacks aside as I desperately tried to lay my hands on my dagger. "Where is it?"

"Where's what?" Jax asked from right behind me, making me jump.

"Holy shit, Jax! Don't do that."

"Do what? What's going on?" He stood with his fists balled at his waist as he stared at me like I'd lost my mind.

"It's Charlotte. She's in trouble and I need my dagger, only it's not—"

"It's there." Jax pointed at the side table right next to the door and then indicated the second shelf.

"Thank the goddess." I grabbed it and then ran out the door.

By the time Jax got his ass to the car, I had my SUV started and was already backing out of the driveway.

"You weren't going to wait for me?" Jax asked, out of breath as he climbed into the passenger seat.

I took off down the road, barely casting him a glance. "Sorry, Jax. I'm just so worried about her. Charlotte might be dramatic sometimes, but she wouldn't cry wolf. Sending 911 texts means she's in serious trouble."

Jax held on with white knuckles as I sped down to the local beach and screeched to a stop. We were out of the SUV in seconds, both of us running toward the outcroppings known as the Mother Stones. The large boulders were shaped in a way to make them look like an older lady who was watching over the town.

Running on the beach wasn't something I did often, so it didn't take long for my calves and lungs to start burning. Sweat broke out over the back of my neck, and the wind was whipping my hair so hard it was obscuring my vision, but nothing was going to keep me from finding my sister.

We rounded a bluff and the Mother Stones appeared against the horizon. But the entire beach seemed to be deserted. By unspoken agreement, Jax and I both stopped running and started to study the area for any potential clues about what might have happened to my sister.

"Where is she?" Jax asked.

I knew he wasn't expecting me to answer. He was just voicing the same frustration that I felt. This was where she was supposed to be, but there was nobody. Only footprints. Both human and canine. "If we knew which prints were hers, we could follow them," I said desperately.

"Or look for Minx's tiny paws. She went with Charlotte, right?" Jax asked.

"I'm sure Charlotte took her. She always does." I started to scan the sand for tiny dog prints that might have been left by a chihuahua.

"Over here!" Jax called. He was staring at the sand, and he hurried to follow a single set of human prints that lined up with those of a small dog.

I fell into step beside him, deciding I didn't have time for any other plan. Charlotte's life wasn't negotiable.

"This way," Jax said, pointing toward a cave in the rocky cliffside.

With one hand carrying the dagger and my other tucked

into Jax's, I let him lead me into the unknown. My head was telling me it was dumb to walk into a cave. That a trap might be waiting. But when images played through my mind of Charlotte being captured, trapped, or something worse by three men, there was no stopping me.

"I'll go first," Jax said, stepping in front of me.

"Hell no. I'm the one with the dagger." I held it up as if to prove my point.

"Marion—"

"Forget it. I'm going in." I wasn't sure why I was insisting, other than I was the one with magical powers. And I figured if something was waiting to ambush us, I'd have the better chance of defending us.

Jax let out a huff of irritation. "Fine. But I'm right behind you."

I nodded once and then stepped into the cave. It took a moment for my eyes to adjust to the pure darkness. When shadows and shapes were visible, I moved further into the cave, feeling as if I'd just walked us into a death trap. Every nerve was on edge. Charlotte had to be somewhere. If not here, then where?

"Marion!" my sister cried, her voice piercing the air. "Watch out!"

But it was too late. Three large canines jumped out of the shadows, coming right for me with their teeth bared.

Instinctively, I held the dagger up in front of me and yelled, "No!" Light streamed from the jewel embedded on the handle, sending the dogs—no, *wolves*—scattering. One hit the side of the cave. Another landed on his head and rolled numerous times before coming to a stop. But the third one just jumped out of the way briefly and then came straight for us again. I once again held up my dagger, but before I could voice the command, the wolf knocked me out of the way and went straight for Jax, his jaws sinking into Jax's neck.

"Jax!" I cried and jumped on the wolf, beating its head with the hilt of my dagger until the creature finally let go. It turned its jaws toward me, but I was ready for him. Instead of using the light to repel him, I buried the steel blade right into the shoulder of the wolf.

He immediately went limp at my feet. "Who's next?" I cried, holding the bloody weapon up high over my head.

The other two wolves scrambled back toward the opening of the cave, both of them howling as if something precious had been taken from them.

"Serves you right," I muttered.

"Marion!" Charlotte called as she ran toward me and seemed to instinctively reach for the dagger I was still holding. No doubt she was thinking the same thing I was. If the remaining two wolves came back, we'd have a lot more power to fight them off together.

But no wolves returned. The only sound in the cave was the low moan coming from Jax.

We both turned at the same time and spotted Jax on the cave floor, his hand covering the gaping wound on his neck with Minx whimpering beside him.

I immediately dropped to my knees, taking Charlotte with me. Together, we placed the dagger's steel blade against Jax's neck.

Charlotte and I looked at each other. We both had tears

in our eyes. We weren't healers and I had no idea if the dagger would work, but we had to try because there was no question that without immediate help Jax's life was in grave danger.

"Goddess of water, of life, of earth, and of creatures," I chanted. "Please help this man. Use our magic to mend him. Make him whole."

Bright white light filled the cave as magic burst not just from the dagger, but from both me and Charlotte. The magic was so hot I felt as if it was going to scorch my fingerprints off. But I held on, willing the magic to do as I asked. Begging it to save the love of my life.

Suddenly, the light vanished and we were thrust back into darkness.

"Jax!" I cried.

"Marion?" he said so faintly I barely heard him.

Charlotte let out a relieved sigh while I grappled around in the darkness, reaching for him. "Jax, thank the gods."

"What happened?" he asked.

"What happened?" I echoed, unable to process anything. It had all happened so fast I barely even knew.

Light appeared, shining right in my eyes. I grimaced and jerked back.

"Sorry," Charlotte said.

When my eyes focused, I saw that she had turned on the flashlight feature on her phone.

"Smart," I said. Then I turned to Jax and gasped.

"What?" he asked, sitting up right beside me.

"Your neck, it's…" I turned wide eyes on my sister.

"It's what?" he asked, pressing his hands to his neck.

"It's not bleeding, but..." I swallowed hard. "The wound... It's angry." That was an understatement. All around it there were dark thin spiderweb veins that meant one thing.

He'd been cursed.

CHAPTER 15

"We have to get him to the hospital," Charlotte said as we both helped Jax to his feet. Minx ran in a circle around Jax, her little body shaking with anxiety.

"No, a healer," I said, shaking my head at her.

"I think this requires more than—" Charlotte froze as she looked around the cave floor. "Where is it?"

"Where's what? The dagger?" I reached down and picked it up where I'd left it near my feet.

"No. The wolf," she said, her voice barely audible. Minx stood right where the wolf had been and started to bark.

"Minx, that's enough, sweet pea," Charlotte said. The dog immediately stopped barking and sat at her feet, her wide eyes shining in the darkness.

I blinked and scanned the cave floor. The inky darkness made it impossible to see clearly. After fumbling around in my pocket, I found my phone and turned on the flashlight feature.

Nothing.

No wolf.

No men.

"It's gone," I confirmed.

Jax let out a groan and stumbled, landing on one knee.

"Jax!" I cried and tugged him back up. He was unsteady on his feet and leaning almost all of his weight on me. "We have to get you out of here."

"Okay," he said weakly.

Minx ran up to him and sniffed his leg.

"I'll be okay, Minx. We'll be back at our walks soon enough," he said, trying to smile at the dog, but it came out as a grimace.

Charlotte hurried over to his other side and wrapped his arm over her shoulders. "We've got you, big guy. As soon as we get you to the car, we'll get you help."

Jax grunted in reply, and although he was still unsteady, the three of us managed to make it to the entrance of the cave with Minx following behind us. There was a small drop from the cave to the sand, which meant I'd have to let him go while I jumped down.

"I'll go first," I said, leaving Jax leaning against the cave wall while Charlotte held onto him with both arms.

"Go on. I'll be fine," Jax said, but his jaw was clenched and his hands were balled into fists. He didn't look fine at all.

But if we were going to get him help, we had to get off this beach. I quickly jumped down and turned just in time to see Jax's face turn completely white. He tried to take one step toward the ledge and then went down hard right in front of me. He landed with a thud on his shoulder, bounced off the edge of the low cliff, and landed sprawled in the sand at my feet.

"Holy shit," Charlotte said, staring down at him with wide eyes. Minx stood at the edge, barking incessantly, no doubt trying to rouse Jax with her high-pitched demand.

Charlotte scooped the dog up, shushing her quietly.

I couldn't blame Minx, I wanted to yell out, too. Demand for him to get up, show us all that he was okay. I knelt down, pressing my shaking hand to Jax's chest, and was relieved to feel his heart beating against his ribcage. "Jax?" I searched his face for any signs he was alert, but his eyes were closed, and when I tried to shake him, he remained unresponsive. My adrenaline kicked in, and while pressing my hand to the side of his face and begging him to wake up, I pulled out my phone and called 911.

"I'd probably pass out after being bitten by a wolf, too," Charlotte said, falling to her knees beside me.

I just nodded and gave the details of our location to the 911 operator.

My sister pulled her sweater off, folded it up, and then gently lifted Jax's head and placed the makeshift pillow underneath. Then she grabbed his hand and held it with both of hers while she whispered, "Goddess of healing and love, we need you now. Please give this man strength to get through this. He saved me. He's a hero." Her voice cracked as she added, "He's worthy."

Tear stung my eyes as I listened to her beg the goddess to help the only man I'd ever loved. Minx curled up next to me, instinctively knowing that I needed support.

"They're coming, Jax," I whispered to him. "Wherever you are, hold on, okay?"

Jax didn't move other than the slow rise and fall of his chest. I watched, holding on to that sign. He was alive and breathing. His heartbeat was strong. He'd get through this. He had to. I couldn't even contemplate a life without him in it. A sob got caught in my throat and I closed my eyes, willing myself to get it together. Falling apart now wasn't an option.

I used all of my energy focusing on Charlotte's chant as we waited.

I wasn't sure how much time had passed, but eventually I laid my head down on Jax's chest, sealing my ear over his heart and listening to its steady beat as I silently prayed to every god and goddess I could think of.

"Here they come, Marion," Charlotte finally said.

I didn't move. I couldn't. That rhythm of his heartbeat was the only thing holding me together.

"Ma'am," a man said from just above me. "We can take it from here."

I let Charlotte guide me away from Jax, my insides hollow. Never in my life had I felt so helpless before.

"What happened to his neck?" the paramedic asked.

"He was bitten by a wolf." Charlotte answered for me and then grabbed Minx, who had started to growl at the first responder in her attempt to protect Jax.

The paramedic frowned and his dark eyes filled with confusion. "That's a bite?"

Charlotte gripped my hand again. "We tried to heal him." She cleared her throat. Then in a quieter, unsure tone, she added, "We have magic."

"I see." The paramedic pressed his lips into a thin line in a show of clear disapproval. "I wish you hadn't done that."

"He'd have bled out if we hadn't," I insisted, remembering the pool of blood we'd left in the cave. "Alive is better than the alternative."

He nodded once and went back to working on Jax. The pair of them had done a quick assessment, got him strapped to a board, and were busy preparing to inject him with something.

"What's that?" I asked.

"It's called R12."

Charlotte and I exchanged a confused look. I swallowed the lump in my throat. "What does it do?"

"It counteracts the lingering effects of magic. It's quite possible you put your husband into a coma with your overzealous actions."

"He's not—never mind." Who cared if this judgmental man thought we were married? And honestly, as annoyed as I was at his disdain for both me and Charlotte for daring to use magic to save Jax, all that mattered was Jax's health. If this man could help him, then he could judge me all he wanted. I just didn't care.

The paramedic locked eyes with his partner. "Ready?"

The other one nodded and started to count. When he got to three, they both lifted the board at the same time, neither of them breaking a sweat. Together they took off down the beach at a decent clip, forcing me and Charlotte to rush after them.

CHAPTER 16

"Someone needs to report that paramedic," Charlotte complained, absently petting Minx's head. We were sitting in the waiting room of the emergency room in Premonition Pointe. Technically she wasn't supposed to have Minx inside the building, but the nurses had relented when Charlotte promised to take her home just as soon as we had news about Jax's condition.

"Report him for what? Being judgmental?" I asked, rubbing my temples. We'd been sitting on the hard plastic chairs for over an hour, and my patience was running thin.

"Yeah," she huffed out. "We're not the only witches in this town. In fact, I'd venture to say without us, there'd be a whole hell of a lot more problems than they can deal with. Look at all the stuff the coven has done to help this town. You'd think people would be grateful instead of rude and just plain ugly. Jax could've died—"

"Charlotte," I said, closing my eyes and shaking my head

as if that would dislodge her words. "Not now, okay? I'm having a hard enough time keeping calm as it is."

"Sorry." There was silence for a few moments before she said, "Maybe I should take Minx home."

I glanced over at her and the little dog curled up in her lap. "No. Not yet. Not until Ty and Kennedy get here."

"Oh. Okay," she said with a solemn nod. "I'll stay."

"Thanks." I glanced over at her, noting that she was biting her cuticles.

"Char?" I asked.

"Hmm?" Her eyes were wide as she looked at me, her thumb still pressed to her mouth.

I reached up and gently lowered her hand so that she was no longer gnawing on her thumb. "Are you okay?"

Her knee started to bounce. "Yeah. I mean, I'm not the one lying in the emergency room, right?"

I took a long look at her. She was sitting on the edge of her seat, one hand now gripping the arm of her chair so tightly her knuckles were white and the other one shaking as she absently petted Minx's head.

I slowly reached out and covered her shaking hand. "You're coming down from your adrenaline rush, and you're still in shock."

"I'm fine," she insisted.

"I know you *will* be fine, but right now I think we need to take care of you." I stood. "I'll go get you something to drink and try to find you something to eat."

"I'm not really hungry," she said.

"I know, but it will help. I promise." Grateful to have something to do besides worry about Jax, I gave her shoulder a quick squeeze and hurried off down the hall in search of the cafeteria.

Ten minutes later, I returned with a plastic cup of orange juice, a turkey sandwich, and a large chocolate chip cookie. Sitting beside my sister, I handed her the food and then scooped Minx off her lap. The warmth of the small dog soothed my frayed nerves, and I was suddenly glad the nurses had let her stay. No doubt she'd been good for Charlotte, too.

After Charlotte got a few bites of food in her system, I asked, "What happened back there at the beach? Why did those men come after you?"

Charlotte put the sandwich down and carefully wiped her fingers before turning to me with a serious expression. "Are you sure you want to hear this right now? We can wait until after we know what's going on with Jax."

"No, I don't want to wait. What happened?"

She took a long sip of the orange juice and then put the food to the side on another chair. "Minx and I were just walking down the beach when I had a feeling I was being watched. The beach appeared deserted, but then I felt a prickle on my neck and I just knew."

"I hate that feeling," I said. "What did you do?"

"At that point, I stopped and glanced around, but I didn't see anything. I was going to brush it off, chalk it up to some sort of strange leftover energy, but Minx wouldn't go any further. When I told her to come with me, she just wouldn't. That's when I knew something was really wrong." Charlotte glanced down at Minx. "She's a good girl."

"She is," I agreed.

"I decided we needed to immediately leave the beach,

but we didn't even get ten feet before three men popped out from behind an outcropping of stones. They surrounded us. There were two larger guys who looked like they might be related. Both with the same build, the same dark curly hair and angular features. The third one was shorter, more polished, like a guy who knew his way around an office. Anyway, he appeared to be the leader. He told me to stop digging around into Sara's case."

"What?" I asked, confused. "Some guy you didn't recognize was telling you to let it go?"

She nodded and then gave me a wry smile. "And you know me. I don't take kindly to men who try to tell me what to do."

"I do know you," I agreed. "So, what did you do next?"

"Well, I told them to go fuck themselves."

I suppressed a groan.

"Oh, come on, Marion. You'd have done the exact same thing and you know it," she said, her eyes narrowed in challenge.

"Maybe, but I'd probably have been more tactful about it."

She snorted. "Do you think they would've cared one iota about tact? Please, Marion, they were threatening to haul me off by my hair."

"Bastards," I muttered.

"That's what I said." She nodded firmly. "Anyway, when I refused to promise to, quote, 'keep my fat ass out of their business,' they obviously didn't like that much. That's when they came after me."

"What did you do?"

"I ran, obviously." She glanced down at Minx and then bent to give the chihuahua a kiss on the head. "It's Minx who gave me a good enough head start that I was able to call you for help. She darted out in front of them and bit the ankles of at least two of them while I put out the SOS." She frowned and then closed her eyes for along moment. "But then they tried to hurt my baby, and I had to go back for her."

I pressed a hand to my abdomen, fearful for what might have happened to both of them.

"I got there just in time before they…" She choked up and wiped at the tears shining in her eyes. "Well, I stopped them from doing the unthinkable."

I didn't want to ask, but there was no holding back. "How did you stop them?"

"I promised to do what they asked if they'd leave Minx alone."

"Okay," I said slowly. "What happened after that?"

Her frown deepened. "They decided they needed to wait for you so that they could deliver the message to you, too. That's when they grabbed me by the hair and pulled me into the cave."

"Those bastards laid their hands on you?" Fire came to life in my belly. No one touched my sister. No one. Those bastards were going to pay. One way or another, I'd track them down and… do what? Curse them? No, I wouldn't do that, but I could hand them over to Brix if he ever reappeared from his undercover stint. Or I could leave things to Sebastian and his crew. They'd find some way of dealing with taking out the trash.

"I got a good punch in on the one in charge," she said

with a tiny, pleased smile. "He won't be making any babies anytime soon."

I couldn't help it. I let out a bark of laughter. Leave it to my sister to maim her attacker where it counted.

She shrugged one shoulder and then frowned as if she were in thought. "You know what I don't understand?"

"What's that?"

"One minute they were there, and then they weren't. I don't know where they went. All I know is that I was getting ready to run out of the cave to find you when the wolves appeared and held me back until you and Jax arrived."

"Maybe the wolves were their plan the entire time," I reasoned. "To get us trapped and then unleash them on us?"

"Maybe," she agreed. "But I don't understand why they didn't threaten you. They spent a lot of time telling me all about how they'd come for everyone I love, including you, Dad, and Denver, all just to get me to say I'd stop putting my nose in their business. They specifically held me to get to you, and then they didn't even try to threaten you. Don't you think that's kind of suspicious?"

It did sound off. "Maybe they weren't expecting Jax. That would have made it three on three. Or three on three and a quarter if we include Minx." I smiled softly down at the pup. She really had turned out to be a lovely addition to my household, even if she had tried to eat Jax's junk the first time they'd met. It was a small miracle that the two had become such good friends. In the beginning, Minx hadn't wanted anything to do with Jax.

"The small one did seem like a dipshit who'd be afraid of anyone who could bench more than forty pounds."

I chuckled. "We'll work on identifying them once we get home. And with any luck, we'll find a way to make sure they're locked up and don't get to touch another woman for many years to come."

"I'd rather castrate them, but I guess your plan works, too," Charlotte said with conviction.

"Ouch," a familiar voice said from behind us. "Remind me never to get on your bad side."

I turned and spotted Ty and Kennedy standing behind us. Ty placed his hand on my shoulder, and I covered it with one of mine, grateful for the support.

"Oh, Ty, baby. You could never piss me off so badly that I'd consider a permanent change of your anatomy," Charlotte said with a smile. "It's just not in your nature."

"Thank the gods for that," Kennedy said, giving me a what-the-hell look.

I gave him a tiny shrug. "It's been a rough day. Charlotte is working through her trauma by imagining what she'd do to her attackers if she had the chance. Don't worry. She's not serious."

"The hell I'm not," she said. "If I have a bald patch on my head from where he dragged me across that cave floor, he'd better be in hiding, like some sort of witness protection. 'Cause I'll hunt his ass down and make good on my promise."

"No one messes with Charlotte's hair," Kennedy confirmed. "They're liable to lose a limb."

"I work hard to keep it looking this good." She pushed up the ends as if to fluff her gorgeous red locks. "They'd deserve it."

Someone cleared their throat. "Miss Matched?"

I twisted back around to stare directly at the doctor who'd been assigned Jax's case. "Yes?"

The tall woman with serious gray eyes stared down at me with judgment radiating from her very pores. "If you don't mind me interrupting the party, I thought you might want an update on Jax Williams, your fiancé."

"Fiancé?" Ty echoed but hushed when Charlotte punched his arm.

As if none of that was suspicious. I forced myself to ignore my family as I focused on the doctor.

"He is your fiancé, right?" the doctor asked, staring pointedly at my bare left ring finger.

"Yes. The ring is being resized," I lied. I'd only told them we were engaged because I was terrified they wouldn't let me see him.

"Riiiight." She gave a quick shake of her head as if she was done thinking about our situation and then said, "Come with me. Mr. Williams is asking for his *girlfriend*."

"I'm sure he's just confused after everything he's been through today. The engagement... It's new."

"Honestly, Miss Matched, I don't care. The patient is asking for you, and he has no immediate family who can be here. So go in, talk to him, but don't wear him out. You can convince the nurses later that you're his fiancé. But if he talks, you're screwed."

"Uh, okay," I said lamely, wondering exactly how the doctor knew the truth. Was I that easy to read? And yet, she was still letting me see Jax. I guessed she meant it when she said she didn't care about the rules, only her patients.

I read the sign over the door. *Intensive Care Unit.*

My head swam. If he was still in the ICU, he was still

critical. My chest felt hollow, like my heart had followed Jax and was no longer in my body.

When we were just outside Jax's door, I stopped abruptly and turned to the doctor. "What will I see in there?"

"Your fiancé," she said dryly and then spun around. "Be quick, Miss Matched. You don't want to wear him out while he's healing."

"Right." I watched her walk down the hall for a few feet and then walked into Jax's room.

As soon as I closed the door behind me, I turned and let out a small gasp.

"Marion?" Jax croaked out in a groggy voice. "You're here?"

"I am," I said, moving to get closer to him. "For as long as you need. But you might want to tell the nurses I'm your fiancé. It just made it easier to get in."

"Fiancé, huh? That doesn't sound so bad."

I was standing near the side of his bed, frozen in place as I stared in utter shock at his wound.

"Marion? What is it?"

I shook my head, unable to answer. Did he know? Had he seen his wound yet?"

"How bad is it?" he asked.

"You don't know?"

He shook his head and winced at the pain. "Tell me."

I couldn't. Not then. Not while he was in the ICU.

"Marion, if you don't tell me, I'm going to get up and look myself."

I groaned and squeezed my eyes shut. And when I opened them, I gave it to him straight. "Your neck, back, and shoulders are covered in inky black veins." But there was a new development. Now the veins had a dreaded purple outline.

"I suppose that means it's bad?" he asked, sounding too tired to even think.

"It's bad, Jax. Very bad."

"A curse?" he guessed.

"Yes. An unbreakable one."

CHAPTER 17

I sat beside Jax's bed, clutching his hand and holding my breath as his eyes fluttered open. "Hey. Welcome back."

He blinked a few times and then turned his head as the door creaked open.

Charlotte poked her head in the door. "Is the coast clear?"

"Of what?" I asked, frowning at her.

"Everyone." She glanced around the room and then quickly slipped in, closing the door behind her. Minx's head popped up out of her sweater. "How are you doing, Jax?"

He shook his head slightly and then turned his attention back to me.

"This is my fault," I said, my voice cracking as I stared into Jax's wide eyes. "If Charlotte and I hadn't jumped in with our magic from the dagger, this never would have happened."

Charlotte let out a derisive huff, and I knew she wanted

to challenge me but likely stayed quiet because she didn't want to start a fight in front of Jax.

Jax tried to speak, but no words came out. He cleared his throat, and finally with a raspy voice, he said, "I think you saved me."

"We did," Charlotte chimed in, her face set in a fierce expression. "We did the best we could under the circumstances. You have to know that, Marion."

Intellectually, I knew she was probably right. I just couldn't ignore the fact that Jax was suddenly cursed. How else would that have happened if not for our magic? The men on the beach hadn't cast any spells. I'd have felt the lingering effects if they had. And the wolf... Was it possible the curse had come from him? I shook my head. There was, of course, a lot of lore revolving around wolves, but it wasn't like I'd ever witnessed anything that could prove those stories true. At least not until now.

The truth was, I was just too afraid to voice my fears. If the curse had come from me and my sister, then purple outline or no, I was determined that we could find a way to reverse it.

"You should call the coven," Charlotte said, clutching Minx to her chest.

I nodded.

The door opened, and in strode a no-nonsense nurse. She wore navy blue scrubs and had her hair pulled back in a severe bun. "Who let that dog in here? This is the ICU," she barked. "Out. Now."

Minx let out a little whimper and strained her head toward Jax. No doubt the little dog wanted to check on him herself.

"We're going, jeez. No need to be bitchy about it," Charlotte muttered.

"This is a hospital, not a doggie daycare," the nurse said with a sniff of superiority.

"Haven't you ever heard of animal therapy?" Charlotte asked, deliberately walking over to Jax's bed and putting Minx in the crook of his arm.

Minx immediately snuggled up next to him and placed her little head on his chest.

Jax closed his eyes and placed his hand on her small body.

"Ma'am, you cannot—" the nurse started, at the same time Charlotte said, "See! Minx is—"

"Stop!" I cried, cutting them both off. "The dog is comforting him. Just let her stay for a few minutes, and then I'll send her home with my sister."

"This is not acceptable," the nurse said, spinning on her heel and stomping out of the room.

Charlotte laughed.

I glared at her. "You're not helping."

"Come on, Marion. You and I both know Minx is exactly where she needs to be."

We both glanced at Jax and then at the vitals monitor. His heart rate had come down, and it did appear that Minx had done more for him than all the medical intervention he'd had in the past hour.

"Minx stays," Jax said without opening his eyes.

Charlotte raised one eyebrow at me.

"Okay. Minx stays," I echoed. I was determined that whatever Jax needed, that's what he'd get.

Five minutes later, when the doctor walked in with the

militant nurse, I was prepared for the fight. But she took one look at the monitor printouts and then turned to the nurse. "Did you give Mr. Williams any meds while you were just in here?"

She shook her head. "No. I was just going to check his IV and his… *infection*, when I encountered the canine issue and then went to find you."

"Right. Then the dog stays as long as they want." The doctor gave me a definitive nod. "Just make sure she stays in this room and doesn't disrupt any of the other patients."

"I will," I said, grateful for her willingness to bend the rules. Both Jax and Minx were calmer since Minx had joined him on the bed.

"Now, let's see how you're doing." The doctor walked over to Jax, checked the IV, and then inspected the curse. As far as I could tell, it remained unchanged. She made a note on the chart and then checked his temperature. Frowning, she wrote down a number. After a thorough inspection, she turned to me. "He's stable. His temperature is elevated, but his heart rate is back to normal, so that's a good sign. Assuming the infection doesn't spread in the next few hours, he'll be moved to a regular room."

It irritated the crap out of me that they kept referring to his curse as an infection. I'd already told them it was a curse, but they'd said medically the dark lines meant an infection, whether cursed or not. They had administered antibiotics, but as far as I could tell, that was just a precautionary measure since he'd been bitten by a wolf. They'd also started the protocol for rabies just in case.

"Thank you," I said to the doctor as she pushed the door open.

"You're welcome."

When the door closed behind the doctor, the nurse turned her glare on me.

"Do not leave that dog here unattended," the nurse said. "Or I'll call animal control."

Charlotte rolled her eyes, and I was grateful she didn't let the nurse bait her.

"We'll manage the dog," I assured the nurse. Then I gave her a sickly-sweet smile. "Thank you for helping us resolve this situation."

She let out an irritated huff and stomped out of the room.

"You're a badass when you want to be," Charlotte said. "Props, big sis."

I waved her off and went to sit by Jax again. His eyes were closed and his breathing was steady, indicating that he'd fallen asleep. *Good.* He needed his rest. "Will you stay with him and Minx?" I asked Charlotte. "I need to make a phone call."

"You got it." She hurried to take a seat on the other side of Jax's bed where she could pet Minx.

I silently left the room and then called the coven.

"IT's A CURSE ALL RIGHT," Gigi said once she came out of Jax's room. He'd been moved out of the ICU about an hour ago, and Gigi, Iris, and Carly had arrived not long after. The other three were busy at their respective jobs and hadn't been able to make it, but they said they'd meet us at the coven circle later if they were needed.

"Let's take a walk," I said, feeling uncomfortable having this conversation while other people were present in the hallway.

"Yes, please," Gigi said, and the three of us followed her out of the hospital and over to a small grassy area where we found a couple of benches and picnic tables. After we sat at one of the tables, Gigi asked, "Can you tell us exactly what happened?"

I took a deep breath and started at the beginning. When I got to the part about wolves suddenly appearing, Carly let out a small gasp and covered her mouth, her eyes wide with horror. "What?" I asked her.

"Wolves? Here in Premonition Pointe?" She grimaced, a pained expression on her face. "That's the curse. Not whatever you and Charlotte did."

I blinked at her. "I'm sorry. I don't know what you're talking about."

"Wolves." She leaned in and lowered her voice. "Werewolves. If Jax was bitten by a wolf and now he has a curse, it seems obvious to me."

"There's no such thing as werewolves," Iris said, her tone sounding anything but sure.

"Werewolves?" Gigi asked, tapping her finger to her chin. "What was it the goddess said when she possessed Marion?"

"Beware of those who walk under the moon," I said automatically. That line had been running through my head for two days straight. A sinking feeling materialized in my gut. "Werewolves. I just…" I squeezed my eyes shut and shook my head. "Is it possible that werewolves are real?"

"Magic is real," Gigi said.

"We're living proof that witches are a reality. And we just spoke to a goddess a couple of days ago," Carly said. "Why wouldn't werewolves be real?"

That wasn't a question I could answer.

"How would we know for sure?" I asked, glancing around at my coven mates.

None of them had an answer.

"Does this mean Jax will turn into a wolf?"

"I really don't know," Carly said. "I've just heard rumors that they exist. No one has ever given me details."

The other two agreed.

My mind raced with a hundred other questions. Would it be painful? Could he survive a transition? Would a pack claim him? Would I have to lock him up in a cell like they did on all the television shows to make sure he didn't tear anyone apart during a full moon? But I didn't voice them. None of us knew anything. And honestly, the werewolf talk was just speculation.

"It's still possible that whatever Charlotte and I did caused this, right?" I asked, clinging to hope. "I never saw anyone shift into a wolf. There were three men who harassed Charlotte, but once I got there, I only saw wolves. She didn't see anything either."

My three coven mates all shared a skeptical glance. I knew what they were thinking. Three men, three wolves. It all added up, right? Yet how had I reached almost fifty years old and never knew that werewolves might be real? If that was true, what about vampires? Did I suddenly have to start worrying about some thousand-year-old dead guy feeding off me?

"Marion, you're spiraling," Iris said, putting her arm

around my shoulders. "We all know that anything is possible right now. The only thing we can do is try to figure out who threatened Charlotte at the beach and why. Maybe then we'll find some answers."

"Everything is falling apart," I said, knowing that I sounded hopeless. Earlier in the day, I was ready to take on the world. Now, all I wanted to do was curl up next to Jax and will him to heal. I had magic. It could happen.

It could, I told myself, no matter how unlikely.

"You should call Brix," Iris urged. "If anyone knows anything about werewolves, it'll be him."

"I can't. He's away right now on a case." I rested my elbows on the wooden table and held my head in my hands. "I don't trust anyone else at the Magical Task Force. If this information got into the wrong hands…"

Carly nodded solemnly. "On that note, I think you should get Jax checked out of the hospital sooner rather than later. If someone makes the same connection we did, then who knows what might happen with that information?"

"You're right." I stood and smoothed my hair back, tying it up with a ponytail holder. "I'm gonna do everything I can to get him home. Will you guys be available to try some spells later this evening?"

They all nodded.

"Thanks. Stay tuned." Determined to keep Jax safe, I strode back into the hospital with purpose. When I reached the end of the hall, a tall dark-haired man hurried out of his room.

A very familiar one.

Carson Kirkwood, Ty's brother.

What in the hell was he doing in Jax's room? Had he come with Ty?

Carson glanced up, spotted me at the end of the hall, and then abruptly spun around and hurried down the hall in the opposite direction.

"Wait!" I called and ran after him. He was too fast, and when he turned a corner, it took me too long to catch up. By the time I was peering down that hallway, Carson was nowhere to be found.

I glanced both ways, making sure I hadn't just missed him somehow. But the hallways were deserted. His panicked escape made me certain, deep in my soul, that Carson was trouble. He wasn't in Premonition Pointe to meet Ty. He was here for some other reason. And I was damned sure going to find out why.

After hustling back to Jax's room, I burst in, half expecting to find something awful, but instead, Jax was sitting up in bed, trying to get his IV out. Charlotte and Minx were nowhere to be found, and I assumed Charlotte had finally taken her dog home.

I cleared my throat. "Going somewhere?"

"Anywhere but here," he said.

I walked over to him and helped him removed the heart monitor. "Any particular reason why?"

"You and I both know they can't help me here." Once he was free of the IV and monitor, he stood, looking surprisingly steady on his feet. The curse was still there, black veins and purple outline, but his color was normal, and he had a hell of a lot more energy than he'd had before his nap.

"Jax?"

"Yeah?" He looked up from where he'd been rummaging around in his pile of clothes.

"What did Carson want?"

"Oh, nothing. He dropped off some cookies from Ty." Jax held up a white paper bag. An *empty* paper bag.

"You ate them already?" I asked, frowning. If all he'd done was drop off cookies, why had Carson run the other way when he saw me?

"Of course I did. Have you seen what they try to pass off as food in this joint?" He pulled his shirt on and finished buttoning his jeans.

"No, thank the gods."

"Lucky you." He shoved his feet into his shoes and then walked over to the door, holding it open for me. "Ready?"

I actually chuckled. He'd spent the last several hours in some state of shock and now he was upright, fully alert, and holding doors open for me. Jax Williams was full of surprises. I walked over to him, kissed him on the cheek, and said, "I've never been more ready."

CHAPTER 18

"I don't need the coven to try to cure me," Jax insisted as we walked into my house. "I feel fine."

"But you've been cursed, Jax. That's clear. We need to figure out what it is and how it will affect you," I said, following him to the kitchen.

"Right now, the only thing I need is some food." He pulled open the refrigerator door and rummaged around until he found a package of sliced roast beef and a bottle of beer.

"Are you sure you should be having a beer—"

"Marion," Jax snapped, cutting me off. "I'm fine. Stop worrying."

I leaned against the door jamb and watched as he devoured over a half pound of roast beef and washed it down with not one, but *two* beers. When he opened the second one, he held my gaze, clearly daring me to question him. I held up my hands in surrender. "Fine. Do whatever you want… for now. But don't think I'm not going to get to the bottom of this curse."

"If it's not bothering me, then why does it matter so much?" he asked, sounding dismissive.

In fact, he didn't sound like Jax at all. The man I knew and loved never cut me off or acted as if my worries were unfounded. I understood that he'd had a rough day, but even on Jax's worst days, he was patient and kind. This man? He was dismissive and full of dominance.

Alpha behavior, a voice whispered in the back of my mind.

I quickly pushed that voice aside. Until I had confirmation that werewolves existed, I wasn't letting myself go there.

"It matters because we don't know what that curse will do to you," I said. "I, for one, would like to be prepared instead of just waiting to make sure it doesn't kill one of us."

"Don't you think you're being a little dramatic?" he asked.

"That's always possible, but if you ask me, you're not worrying enough." What I didn't say out loud was that I'd be worrying enough for the both of us.

"If anything seems off, you'll be the first to know." He opened up the fridge and started foraging for more food.

"We're leaving in ten minutes," I called as I walked into the other room.

"I'm not going," he called back.

"Yes, you are," I insisted and then walked out onto my front porch, already scrolling through my contacts. When I found the name I was looking for, I tapped it and sat in the wooden swing, waiting for an answer.

"Marion! It's good to hear from you," Hollister said after picking up.

I sat back, relieved to hear his voice. If anyone had suggestions for a way to cure Jax's curse, it would be him. Hollister owned Crooner's Cauldron, a magical shop in Southern California. "Thank the gods you're there. I need help."

"So, this isn't a social call?" he asked, sounding amused.

"I wish it was." I stared out into the fading daylight and suddenly wanted to scream. Everything had gone to shit. My business was DOA at the moment, Charlotte had been attacked, Ty had been distant ever since his brother walked into his life, and now Jax was cursed. If I wasn't so determined to find a cure for Jax, I would have been tempted to curl up in bed and just sleep until something changed.

"What's going on, Marion?" His tone was serious now. "How can I help?"

"Are werewolves real?" I blurted.

There was silence on Hollister's end.

After a moment, I said, "They are, aren't they?"

"Yes. But they usually don't interact with witches. Did you come across one?"

"Three." My head started to ache, and I wondered when I'd eaten last. But the very idea of food made me nauseated. I pressed my hand to my stomach, willing it to settle.

"Three? Seriously?" Hollister asked, sounding awed.

"Maybe four." My voice cracked and tears stung my eyes, horrifying me. I sucked in deep steady breaths, willing myself to get my emotions under control. I would not break down and cry while I was speaking to Hollister. That was nonnegotiable.

"What does that mean?"

"Jax was bitten."

Hollister sucked in a sharp breath. "And he survived?"

The way he'd asked sounded like that was an unusual thing. "Barely," I admitted. "He was in bad shape when Charlotte and I used our magic from the dagger to close his wound."

"Whoa."

When Hollister didn't elaborate, I asked, "What does that mean?"

"Well, I'm not sure. From what I understand, people rarely survive werewolf bites. The ones who do…"

"You can't just stop there, Hollister. Finish whatever you were going to say," I demanded, already knowing I was going to hate whatever he said next.

"Marion, if he's been cursed to be a werewolf, he's going to need a pack. Without one, he's going to have a rough time of it."

"How? And where in the hell would he find a pack? Surely he can't be expected to run with the people who attacked my sister and then tried to kill him!" My voice had risen, and I was well aware I was starting to sound slightly hysterical.

"He's going to need support when he finally shifts. As far as where to find a pack, I can't answer that. I've only encountered a couple of werewolves, and that was out in the desert."

"This conversation isn't helping me," I complained.

"I'm sorry, Marion. I'm hardly an expert on shifters. Have you called Brix?"

"He's unavailable right now," I said, frustrated that the one time I needed the head of the Magical Task Force, he was completely off the grid.

"I'm sorry I can't be more helpful," Hollister said.

"No need to apologize." I clutched the phone and gazed out at the orange sky as the sun started to go down. "You've given me more than I had five minutes ago. I just don't know what to do with that information."

"I bet. I'll see if I can drum up anything else that might be useful. I could make some phone calls to some acquaintances."

"Would you?" I asked, feeling a tiny weight lift off my shoulders. It felt good to have someone on my side who'd go out of their way to help me and Jax. Not that the coven wouldn't do everything they could. It was just that Hollister was different somehow. His entire life revolved around magic and the unexplained. He knew things the rest of us didn't. The wealth of knowledge he carried was impressive.

"Of course, Marion," he said, his tone soft now. "How's Jax doing?"

"Fine, I guess. He was pretty out of it earlier today, but by late this afternoon, he was up and around and refusing to even try to eradicate the curse, insisting that he could handle whatever is coming his way. Honestly, the stubborn attitude is something I can do without, but there's no denying that physically he's a thousand times better than he was earlier when he was lying on that cave floor nearly unconscious."

"He sounds like a handful right now."

"He is," I agreed. "But he's going to the coven circle whether he wants to or not."

Hollister laughed. "Never change, Marion. You're perfect just the way you are. I'll call you when I have something to report."

"Thanks, Hollister. I really appreciate it." I ended the call and let my head fall back against the wooden swing.

"You're perfect just the way you are?" Jax growled, making me nearly jump right out of the swing.

"Holy hell!" I pressed a hand to my chest as if I were keeping my heart from beating right out of it. "How long have you been standing there? And wait... You heard Hollister through the phone from way over there?"

"You said the two of you were just friends." Jax's eyes flashed with something that looked like pure rage.

"Whoa," I said, standing up and placing my hands out. "What is going on here, Jax? Why are you so angry?"

"That man wants you," he said flatly.

"He doesn't," I countered, trying desperately to keep my cool. Jax hadn't ever acted this possessive before. I had to believe the change had to do with his bite. Was he turning into some sort of alpha asshole right before my eyes because of the bite? "He's going to help me get answers about your curse. For you and for me. That's not a guy who is waiting in the wings for us to break up."

"He's just trying to get close to you so he can be ready when an opportunity arises and he finally has a shot with you."

I couldn't help it. I rolled my eyes. "You're reaching, alpha boy." I walked over and pressed my hand to his chest, placing it right over his rapidly beating heart. "Since when did you decide you no longer trust me?"

Jax placed his hand over mine, clutching it tightly. "I don't know, Marion. I'm not sure where all these feelings are coming from." He took a few deep breaths and buried his head into the crook of my neck. "I just feel, I don't know, sort of crazy."

I buried my free hand into his thick hair and just held on until I heard the rumble of an engine come to a stop in front of my house. Together, we both looked over and spotted Ty and Kennedy climbing out of Ty's SUV.

"Hey, Ty!" Jax called. "Thanks for the cookies today."

"Cookies?" Ty asked. "What cookies?"

"The ones you sent to the hospital. I'm telling you, after eating those, I perked right back up. I guess I just needed a little bit of sugar to get back to my old self," Jax explained.

Old self my ass, I thought, but kept my commentary to myself.

Ty was frowning as he walked over to us. Kennedy followed with Paris Francine trotting beside him, looking adorable with her pink rhinestone harness and matching leash. Ty stopped beside me and glanced between me and Jax. Finally, he met Jax's gaze and said, "I didn't send any cookies. In fact, Kennedy and I were just about to go upstairs and make you some now since we weren't able to earlier. I had a deadline for work. Otherwise, I would have stayed at the hospital to visit you when they moved you out of ICU." Ty craned his neck, trying to see Jax's wound. When he got a good look at it, his face turned very pale.

"He's okay," I reassured Ty. "I promise. We're working on

a way to free him from the curse." It was a small lie. Technically no one was doing anything of the sort, but I had feelers in place. If there was a way to do it, we'd figure it out.

"Yeah, I'm okay, kid," Jax said, sounding nothing like the man I'd fallen in love with. He didn't call Ty kid, and he certainly didn't use that douchey tone either. "Like I said, those cookies made all the difference."

Ty frowned and his brows pinched together in confusion. "I already told you I didn't make cookies, nor did I send any. Where'd you get them?"

"Carson. He said you wanted to come by but that you couldn't get away, so he ran them by."

"Carson?" Ty asked, obviously confused. "How did he even hear about the incident?"

"That's the million-dollar question, isn't it?" I asked, my mind racing. Carson had brought Jax cookies that had seemingly cured Jax of whatever was happening to his body after the bite. And then he'd lied to Jax. Why?

"You really didn't send them?" Jax asked Ty.

Ty shook his head and then looked at Kennedy, who was behind him.

"I didn't send any cookies either," Kennedy quickly confirmed.

"That's too bad," Jax said. "Because I think they may have been the thing that saved my life."

I jerked around to stare at him. "You're saying they were herbal?"

Jax nodded.

"With magic?" I demanded.

"Absolutely. It's been one hell of a ride today."

"Well, I hope you're up for another one, big guy." I

slipped my arm through his and tugged him off the steps. "Because right now we have a date with the coven at the bluff."

Jax groaned. "I told you, I feel fine."

"From the cookies that were laced with something," I said dryly. "Not knowing what they used in their potion means we have a problem. You can either go willingly, or the three of us will take you down and force you. Your choice."

"We will?" Kennedy asked with a tiny squeak.

"I'd like to see you try," Jax said through gritted teeth.

I turned on him, my anger finally overflowing. "Listen up, Jax Williams. I'm tired of this machismo crap. Get in the SUV or get out of my life."

It was a bluff, of course. No way would I let him walk out of my life, not while I was still trying to figure out what had happened to him.

Finally, after a long moment, Jax walked over to my SUV and got in.

Behind the wheel on the driver's side, of course. I pressed a hand to my forehead. "It's going to be a long-ass night, isn't it?"

Ty just patted me on the back. "Good luck."

"Thanks." We were definitely going to need it.

CHAPTER 19

"This isn't the way to the coven circle," I said, peering out the window. The sun had set, and the almost full moon had risen, shining brightly in the sky.

"I know." Jax gave me a cheeky grin.

"Jax!" I turned to stare at him, my fists clenched in my lap. "This is serious."

"Marion," he shot back, offering no explanation or defense for his detour.

Sitting back in my seat, I stared straight ahead, peering at the road. "Where are we going?"

"To have some fun." He turned the SUV down an unmarked road and maneuvered through the curves as if he'd driven them for years.

"You're starting to make me a little nervous, Jax," I said, trying not to let all kinds of horror-filled suspicions take over my mind. If he really was a wolf, would he shift under the full moon? Was that really a thing? "Charlotte isn't going to have to call out the search party for me in the morning, is she?"

Jax glanced over at me and shook his head slightly as he rolled his eyes. "Don't be so dramatic. Just give me an hour and then we'll meet up with your coven. Deal?"

An hour? I could probably manage that, but it would inconvenience everyone who was likely already on their way to the bluff. Plus, even if he wasn't planning anything nefarious, I was going to remain on edge until I knew exactly what was going on with him and whether or not I could fix it. "You know why I'm anxious," I said quietly. "Plus, I don't love leaving the coven hanging like this."

"Marion, I just need to get out of my head for a few minutes. And I wanted to do that with you. If the coven can't wait, I promise we'll see them tomorrow. Is that all right?" he asked, suddenly sounding more like the man I'd fallen in love with instead of the one who'd been acting like some sort of alpha asshole.

My hard edges softened as I recognized the sincerity in his voice. I'd been full speed ahead, trying to fix a problem we didn't even understand yet while he'd been… what? Just trying to cope? Surely, I could give him this one night. "I'll text Iris."

He let out a long, relieved sigh. "Thank you."

"You're welcome," I said as I shot off a text to Iris. A few minutes later, she confirmed that the coven could wait. "They'll still be there in an hour, so we can't stand them up again."

"Understood." Jax pulled the SUV to a stop in a small clearing at the side of the road, killed the engine, and then jumped out of the vehicle. "Let's go, Marion. You're going to miss it."

As he slammed the door, I climbed out of the SUV and glanced around. We were surrounded by redwood trees, but at the end of the road there was what appeared to be a trailhead with a sign that I couldn't read. It was too dark.

"This way." Jax grabbed my hand and tugged me toward the trail.

"I'm not going on a hike in the dark!" I planted my feet, unwilling to indulge his reckless whim.

"We're not hiking." This time instead of tugging me along after him, he swept me up into his arms and took off down the trail.

"Jax? What the hell? Let me down," I demanded, unable to keep the laughter from my lips.

"Nope. Not until we get where we're going."

"Caveman," I said, but my voice didn't hold any heat.

He let out a deep, sexy growl and kept up his swift pace.

I had to admit that even though my head was screaming at me to put a stop to his Neanderthal behavior, I couldn't deny that I was enjoying myself. What hotblooded woman didn't want to be manhandled by her sexy caveman?

It wasn't long before we cleared the trees and ended up on a small beach that looked out over a secluded cove. The sound of the gentle waves crashing along the sand soothed me.

Jax slowly lowered me to my feet and then pulled me against his chest. He had one hand buried in my hair and the other sliding down my waist toward my hip, and I stared into his gorgeous dark eyes just as I had so many times before and let myself get lost in him.

"Jax," I whispered as my gaze traveled down to his lips. "What are you doing?"

"What does it look like I'm doing?" He didn't wait for an answer. Instead, he tilted his head down and roughly claimed my lips with his own. His arm came around my waist, pulling me to him until I was plastered against his hard frame.

I was quickly swept up in his all-consuming kiss. He tasted of vanilla and a hint of chocolate, and I couldn't get enough. As we stood there on the beach, wrapped up in each other, the rest of the world slipped away. All I knew was this man I loved deeply and his rough and tender moments.

"Marion," he whispered against my lips just before he took my mouth again. His hands slipped under my shirt, skimming my skin as they slid up my sides. A shiver rocked my entire body, lighting me up and making me ache for him.

When his lips glided across my jawbone and then down my neck, I tilted my head back, giving him more access.

And when he tugged at my shirt, I let him. The cool night air was a balm on my feverish skin, and when Jax's nimble fingers stripped me of the rest of my clothes, I didn't protest.

Somewhere in the back of my mind, my subconscious was screaming that this was reckless. That we were taking risks that were far worse than just the possibility of being caught having sex on a beach. Jax was cursed. He might be well on his way to becoming a werewolf.

But right then, I just didn't care.

I wanted him. Wanted to forget about everything and

just be together. For now, it was exactly what I needed. What *we* needed.

"Your turn," I said, unbuttoning his jeans.

Jax lowered his gaze and watched as I worked open his fly and pushed his jeans and boxer briefs down. His erection stood tall and proud, straining toward me. When I didn't move to touch him, he grabbed my hand and wrapped it around himself, his eyes closing in sheer pleasure. "I don't think I'll ever get tired of you touching me."

While I gently stroked him, I placed my other hand against his cheek and leaned in to give him a long, lingering kiss. "That's not something you'll ever need to worry about."

"Good." He quickly stripped his shirt off, thrust once into my hand, and then pulled away just long enough to spin me around so that my back was against his chest. He plunged his hand between my legs, finding me wet and ready for him. "Fuck, Marion. No one has ever turned me on like you do."

He crooked his finger, pulling a gasp from my lips when he found just the right spot.

I reached back, grabbing his head and turning into him for a searing kiss.

He played my body with his expert hands, one squeezing my nipple while the other brought me closer and closer to the brink of an orgasm.

The cold was nonexistent. There was only heat and passion between us. The uncontrollable need for him had consumed every inch of my being. I ripped my mouth from his and panted, "Now, Jax. I need you inside of me now."

He didn't hesitate. A low growl rumbled from his lips as he wrapped his arms around my waist and lowered us to the sand. He pushed into me from behind, his larger body covering mine. When he was fully seated, his groin flush with my flesh, we both groaned our pleasure. I loved the full feeling of him inside of me, claiming me.

"You're mine," he said into my ear and then pulled all the way out before slamming back into me.

"Jax!" I cried, loving his dominance and grinding back into him, taking everything he had to give.

Jax held himself in place and ran a soft hand down my spine. "So fucking beautiful in the moonlight," he whispered before planting kisses from my neck to the middle of my back, never once moving his hips.

"Jax, please," I begged, needing him to move.

"What do you want, Marion?" he asked as if it wasn't obvious.

"I need you to fuck me," I said and pressed back into him again.

"Is that right?" he asked with a small chuckle.

I nodded. "If you don't, I'm going to—"

He pumped his hips, slamming into me, sending shockwaves of pleasure pulsing through me. "Going to do what?"

I moaned.

"That's right, baby. I'm the one who knows how to make you feel good." His hands tightened around my hips and suddenly he was holding me still while he pounded into me.

My entire body tingled with pleasure, each thrust driving me more and more wild, the tension nearly unbearable as I begged, "Touch me. Now, Jax. Please."

"I know what you need," he growled into my ear as his arm wrapped around me and cupped my breast, his fingers squeezing my nipple. A lightning bolt of pleasure shot straight to my center, only torturing me more.

"Gods," I panted, pushing back to meet each of his thrusts, desperate for release now. "If you don't touch me, I'll have to do it myself," I warned.

"No." He placed both of his hands over mine, lacing our fingers together in the sand as he continued to pump into me from behind. "Not. Yet."

He was wild, almost out of control as he took me longer and harder than ever before. It would only take one touch, right in that magic spot and then—

Jax bit down on my shoulder right where it met my neck, and suddenly my world exploded into fireworks of color as my body tensed. My toes curled as a tidal wave of the most intense pleasure exploded inside of me, sending tingles all the way to the top of my head, the tips of my fingers, and down to the soles of my feet.

"Fuck, yes!" he cried as he slammed into me one last time and let his own orgasm take him.

CHAPTER 20

*A*fterward, we both collapsed into the sand, panting. Jax rolled over onto his back and pulled me to him until my head was lying on his chest. He didn't say anything. He just ran his hand through my mussed hair and stared up at the sky.

"That was…" I trailed off, not at all sure what to say.

"Incredible," he finished for me.

"Yes, no question," I agreed, but there was more to say, wasn't there? I was pretty sure blowing off the coven and having public sex wasn't exactly on the list of acceptable activities when your partner had just been cursed.

Jax leaned up on his elbow, looked down at me, and grinned. Then without a word, he kissed me once before climbing to his feet and running flat out into the water. He let out a howl before plunging into the waves.

"Holy shit," I muttered as a slight breeze caused gooseflesh to pop out over my exposed skin. I wrapped my

171

arms around myself and watched as Jax's powerful body sluiced through the waves. What was even happening?

I scanned the area, double-checking that we were actually alone, and then walked over to the edge of the water and dipped my toes in.

"Whoa," I whispered and stepped back out of the water.

"Marion, get your gorgeous ass in here!" Jax called as he bobbed in the water.

"Hell no. You're insane." I grinned at him.

"Oh, am I?" He swam back to the shore and walked up to me, dripping wet. "Do you really want to see insane?"

"No, I— Ack!" I cried as he picked me up and carried me into the water. We stopped when he was waist deep with my feet dangling in the surf. "You better not drop me, Jax Williams."

"What happens if I do?" His eyes glinted in the moonlight.

"You're going to have one pissed off witch on your hands," I said sweetly.

He raised one eyebrow.

"Don't you even think— Holy shit!" I cried as I was plunged into the icy cold water. I came up sputtering, ready for a fight.

But Jax wrapped his arms around me, pulling me in close. And even though we were standing in water that I was sure was going to turn my toes blue, his body heat took away the worst of the chill. "It's not so bad, is it?"

"No," I reluctantly admitted. There was something magical about being naked with him in the ocean under the moonlight. "How did you find this place?"

His lips quirked into a mischievous smile. "It's private property. That's why no one is here."

"Beaches aren't private in California," I said, narrowing my eyes at him.

He nodded. "True, but the woods that surround it are, and there's no other way to get to it. So we can come here any time we want, and no one will bother us."

"What about the owner?"

"You're looking at him." He bent his head and nibbled at my neck as he grabbed my butt, pulling me closer to him.

"What?" I jerked back, my eyes wide as I stared at him. "How? When? Why? This land must be worth a pretty penny."

He chuckled. "I'd imagine so, but as it turns out, my great-uncle left it to me. I just found out a month ago. I was going to bring you here on our way up the coast, but our plans got derailed. I couldn't wait another day. How do you feel about living at Midnight Cove?"

"What exactly are you asking, Jax?" I asked carefully. "Because it kind of sounds like—"

"I'm asking you to move in with me," he said, cutting me off. "At least I am when I get a house built. I suspect with permits and the California Coast Commission it could take a few years, but when it's done, there's really no one else in this world I'd want to share it with. What do you say, Marion? Do you think you could stand living with a grumpy construction guy twenty-four-seven?"

Stunned into silence, I didn't answer him for a long moment.

"Marion?" His brow furrowed. "Was that too much too fast?"

His voice snapped me out of my trance. "No! I mean, yes. I mean, no, it's not too fast, and yes, I'd love to live with you on this little cove. I can't think of anything I'd want more."

All the tension seemed to drain out of his shoulders as his eyes lit with happiness. "Really?"

"Really." I reached up and brushed his hair out of his eyes. There was so much up in the air at the moment. Jax's curse, my business, the mystery around the attacks on Sara's dates. This really was no time to be making plans for my future, but the truth was, there was really only one thing I wanted.

Jax.

Everything else in my life, I could rebuild or start over. But what I had with Jax was what I'd been looking for my entire life. Building a home with him, sharing our lives, growing old together no matter what life looked like, that's what I was willing to go all-in on.

There was just one problem.

The curse.

I let my fingers trail over the healed wound and traced the black veins. "I don't ever want to lose you, Jax."

"You won't, baby," he said, hugging me with both arms.

"You're right. I won't. Not if I have anything to say about it." I pulled away from him, met his dark gaze, and then said, "It's time to meet the coven."

This time he didn't protest. He just slipped his fingers into mine, and together, we walked out of the surf, tried our best to dry off with Jax's T-shirt, and got dressed. Twenty minutes later, we arrived at the bluff where the coven was waiting.

"Hey," Hope said as she scanned Jax's bare torso. When

she spoke again, her voice was full of humor. "Where exactly have you two been?"

"I had something to show Marion," Jax said, wrapping his arm around my waist.

"I bet you did," Hope muttered under her breath just loud enough for me to hear it.

I gently jammed an elbow into her side. "Stop."

"Never," she promised, winking at me. "I hope you had a good time."

"I did, thank you," I said as if nothing untoward had happened back at the cove.

Gigi rose from her spot on a piece of driftwood and came over to inspect Jax's curse. She held a white pillar candle up, making the purple outline glow. "I see nothing's really changed."

"Not with the curse, no," I confirmed, but I couldn't help thinking that Jax *had* changed. The man I fell in love with was still in there underneath all the personality shifts I'd seen, but I couldn't deny that whatever the curse was, it had changed him.

"I think it's best to recall the goddess," Gigi said. "We need answers, and I don't feel comfortable trying to reverse a curse when we don't even know what it is."

The rest of the coven agreed.

I felt like I was going to vomit. Being a vessel for the goddess was no picnic. It wasn't something I was eager to repeat. But I'd do it... for Jax. "Yeah. Okay," I agreed and then pulled Jax into the circle with me.

"This isn't going to hurt, is it?" Jax teased.

I let out a humorless bark of laughter. "Only if we're lucky."

His eyes widened with surprise as he jerked his head back to study me. "Are you serious?"

"Yes," I said, and at the same time, the rest of the coven said, "No."

Jax glanced around at them and let out a small chuckle. "I see." He turned to me. "Well, I suppose I'll just have to take my chances."

"Don't say I didn't warn you." I took two candles from Gigi and handed one to Jax.

"What am I supposed to do?" he asked me.

I turned and smiled at him. "Just stand there and look pretty."

He rolled his eyes but got the message. There wasn't anything to do but wait for the coven to do their thing.

The six of them lined up around the circle, each of them holding a white candle. All six of them closed their eyes and waited until Gigi called, "Goddess of Knowledge, we seek your wisdom."

All at the same time, they released their candles, letting them float in the air around me and Jax.

"Whoa," he said.

I nodded to his candle. "Let go."

When I released mine, he let his go as well, and the two candles circled us as if keeping us bound together.

"Goddess of Knowledge, hear our call!" Gigi and the rest of the coven chanted into the night.

Normally, I'd feel a thread of powerful magic sparking around me and growing stronger as the witches chanted, but tonight, there was only the whisper of power. The kind that would float candles but wasn't enough to call a goddess.

Gigi's face scrunched up in concentration as she

continued to call on the goddess. A sheen of sweat had popped out on her forehead, only visible by the floating candlelight.

I could both hear and feel the frustration from the coven.

Jax glanced over at me, frowning. *What's happening?* he mouthed.

I gave him a tiny shake of my head, closed my eyes, and tried to do everything I could to open myself up to the goddess.

Still nothing.

Finally in frustration, Gigi called, "Just send us a sign!"

Lightning struck right at Jax's feet, making him jump backward, and he nearly stumbled right out of the circle. I grabbed his arm with both hands, keeping him inside the barrier.

"Holy shit. No one said anything about a lightning storm," he said. "We have to get out of here."

I shook my head. "No, we don't. It's not a lightning storm. It's the sign Gigi asked for."

The candles slowly floated to the ground, and all six of the coven members stared at Jax's feet.

I followed their gazes and let out a gasp of surprise. Instead of a burned mark, there was an envelope with something scrawled across the front. None of us moved.

Jax glanced at the envelope. "Where did that come from?"

"The goddess. It's a message for you," Gigi said.

He gave her a skeptical look. "Seriously?"

"Yes. It's at your feet. Meant only for you."

Kneeling down, Jax reached for the envelope, but just

when his fingers touched it, the parchment went up into flames, burning into ash right before our eyes. "What the hell?" He jerked his fingers back and held the singed tips against this bare chest.

I grabbed his other hand, holding tight as the smoke rose and curled into letters until it spelled out a message:

You will forever walk under the moonlight.

The message hung there in the air, making it feel as if time had stopped. And then the smoke shattered into thousands of little wisps before it vanished into thin air.

"Does that mean what I think it means?" Iris said, filling the silence.

No one voiced the answer, but the words were right there in my mind, screaming the truth.

Jax was a werewolf.

CHAPTER 21

"*T*his is it! Trace Foster's address," Charlotte said for at least the third time that day.

"I've heard that before," I said from my spot on the couch. I was busy trying to build a relaunch for the dating agency once we figured out who'd actually poisoned the five men who'd gone out with Sara.

Charlotte and I had already met with and dismissed the other three dates the day before. They'd been less than helpful and so far, the only information we'd gotten that might be useful had been from Norman. He was the reason we knew the gift baskets contained goat cheese, and I'd manage to confirm with Sara that she had *not* included it. She'd seemed shocked and slightly appalled that anyone would stuff her basket with cheese, considering she'd recently gone vegan.

"Get your shoes on. We're going," Charlotte said.

"What? I'm not going anywhere," I said. "I'm working on this new plan. And then when Jax gets back from his daily swim, we're heading over to Sebastian's so he can give us an update on the background checks he's done."

Charlotte stood, her hands on her hips. "Seriously? You're going to send me into the lion's den all by myself? What if he attacks me? I can't go out on this mission without my magical partner."

I stared at her, taking in her stern expression and frustrated stance. "You really think you need me? You've done all the talking so far. I've just been a glorified taxi driver."

"Uh, of course I do. Who else is going to save my ass when I get into trouble?" she demanded.

"I'll do it!" Celia, the waif-like ghost, popped into my living room, her big Kewpie doll eyes wide with excitement. "I'm a great wing man. Just ask Marion."

"You? A great wing man?" Charlotte scoffed. "The last time you went anywhere with me, you spent the entire time flirting with a guy who was barely legal. That isn't the kind of help I need."

"Marion!" the ghost demanded. "Tell her how useful I am."

I shrugged one shoulder. "She knows what you're capable of." Celia was a ghost who'd haunted me after she'd died in a car crash while she was on a date with someone I'd chosen for her. Now she worked for me... sort of. She came into the office when she felt like it and was often sent off to keep tabs on people when we needed someone to watch over them. Like when I'd had her keep an eye on Kennedy when he and Ty had moved home and he'd gotten involved with someone who nearly got him thrown in jail. Celia had been right there to alert me when things went south.

"No offense, Celia, but I just really need Marion for this job," Charlotte insisted.

I let out a long sigh. "Can it at least wait until Jax gets back? If I'm going, he'll want to tag along, too."

"You do realize how annoying that is, right?" Charlotte asked.

"It's not annoying to have him come with us. He makes us safer," I insisted. It wasn't that I thought we needed Jax with us. We didn't. Not with our combined magical power. The issue was that I hadn't been able to leave him alone since he'd been bitten. I was still waiting for the other shoe to drop when the consequences of that bite finally reared its ugly head.

"If you say so." Charlotte closed her laptop, grabbed Minx, who was sleeping on the ottoman in front of her, and stalked off to her bedroom.

Celia shrugged. "Give me a shout if you need me." Then the ghost disappeared again.

It wasn't even a minute later when the door burst open and Ty stomped into the house, slamming the door behind him. "We need to talk."

"Okay." I rose to my feet and tilted my head to the side, studying him. Ever since Carson had arrived, Ty had been short with me. For the first time, maybe ever, he wasn't sharing his daily life with me. He was closed off and seemed wary, almost as if he talked to me, he'd find out something else he hadn't known, and he didn't want to deal with it or me. "What do we need to talk about?"

"This!" He waved a manila envelope in the air and stomped into the kitchen.

I stared after him, wondering what in the hell "this" was.

When I heard the chair legs scrape the kitchen floor, I followed him. But instead of sitting down, I moved to the counter to make myself a cup of coffee. I held up a mug. "Want some?"

"No. And this isn't a social call. I don't have time for niceties."

"Uh, okay," I said, not bothering to hide my irritation. "But you're going to have to give me just a second, because with that tone and attitude, I'm definitely not going to make it through this conversation without a giant shot of caffeine." I was both frustrated and concerned by Ty's attitude. He'd never spoken to me in such a defensive tone. We'd always had a close relationship and never had any trouble communicating, but ever since Carson arrived, things had changed.

When I had a full mug of coffee, I contemplated adding a generous dollop of Irish Cream but decided against it. As much as I wanted it, now was not the time for booze. Especially if I was going to head out on a mission with Charlotte later that afternoon. "Okay, I'm here. Ready to talk," I said as I took a seat at the table. "What's wrong? What's in that envelope?"

He ripped the envelope open and slammed a small stack of papers in front of me. "Read it."

I scanned the paperwork, noting that it was paperwork for his trust, the one that Trish had left him. Frowning, I looked up at him. "Where did you find this?"

"Does that matter?" He crossed his arms over his chest and glared at me.

"Why are you mad at me? You're the one who has been going through my paperwork. I'm the one who should be offended," I said, finally letting my frustration fly. "Since when do you go snooping around in my files? You know if you wanted to see this, all you had to do was ask."

"I didn't touch your files," he shot back. "This was left in my mailbox with a sticky note that told me to read page two."

"What's on page two?" I asked, not even bothering to look at it. I knew what the trust said. Hell, I'd been there when Trish had gone to the lawyers. Everything Trish had left him was in that trust, and he could access it for tuition but wouldn't receive the balance until he turned thirty. It was a considerable amount of money, and I'd always thought Trish had been smart to put the age stipulation on it. Ty deserved to find his own way without the cushion of his mother's substantial nest egg. It wouldn't make Ty rich. Or at least not filthy rich, but it would be enough for a house with some left over to start his own business if he wanted or to invest and be able to lead a very comfortable life.

"It says right here that the trust is to be equally split between my mother's children." He stabbed at the paperwork. "It even has Carson's name listed."

"That's just not possible, Ty. I was there in the room when they were explaining the documentation with Trish. I swear to you, this is not the copy she filed at the courthouse."

"Really?" His gaze drifted down to the notarization stamp. "Looks official to me."

"Okay, so if it is, why are you so pissed off at me?" I asked calmly, trying to defuse the situation. "I didn't know about this. I didn't even know about Carson."

He stared at me, and his eyes narrowed.

"Ty?" I asked. "Why would—"

"Stop!" He held a hand up. "You really didn't know? The paperwork you have really doesn't say any of this?"

I got up from the table, walked over to my living room credenza, and unlocked the bottom drawer. It took me a minute to find the document I wanted in the thick folder I'd kept when settling her estate. I scanned it quickly, confirming that I wasn't losing my mind before handing it to Ty.

His face turned pale as he slowly sank into a chair at the kitchen table. When he was done reading, he looked up into my eyes and said, "It only lists me as her son."

I nodded.

"How is that supposed to make me feel?" he spit out. "She just abandoned Carson and then she went and made a legal document that cut him out completely. What kind of mother did I have?"

"One who loved you very much," I said. "Trust me, sweetheart," I soothed as I grabbed his hand and held on. "You were her entire world."

"But not Carson? Why wasn't he part of our world?" Ty asked, obviously struggling with his mother's choices.

"I don't know. It's a mystery to both of us," I assured him. "But one thing I'm sure of is that your mother had her reasons. And if I had to guess, it was to protect both of you."

"How is this protecting Carson?" he demanded. "By leaving him nothing? That makes no sense, Marion."

It made sense to me. I had my suspicions and doubts when it came to Carson, but I didn't want to voice them now. Not without any proof to back them up. Ty would only see it as unfair to his brother instead of me looking out for him and making sure that no one was trying to take advantage of him. Instead, I glanced back at the paperwork and the unmarked manila envelope and asked, "Who do you think put this in your mailbox?"

He shook his head. "No clue."

None? Seriously? "You don't think it was Carson?"

"How would he have this paperwork?" Ty asked.

I had to admit that I didn't have any answers. Only suspicions. "I don't know. But do you mind if I take a look at this? Maybe I'll find a clue as to who sent it to you."

He waved an impatient hand and said, "Please. It's enlightening."

"Enlightening?" I echoed.

He just shrugged.

With my coffee in hand, I quickly skimmed the paperwork and compared it to the copy I had. Besides the addition of Carson, the only other thing that stuck out to me was the date. Ty's mystery paperwork was dated and notarized one month after the paperwork I had.

"Son of a… dammit," I muttered to myself and then clamped my hand over my mouth, trying to stop a whole string of expletives.

"What?"

"This is the valid trust," I said, pointing at his stack of papers. "If they are authenticated, then it overrides the copy I have, and you're going to have to share your nest egg with Carson."

"Okay… and?" he asked.

"That doesn't bother you?"

He shook his head. "He's my brother. I was going to share it anyway."

"Ty, that's really generous. But don't you think we should—"

"No. He's my brother. He gets half," Ty insisted as he got up from the table. He started to walk back toward the front door but paused for just a second to glance back at me. "I'm sorry I yelled at you. This entire experience has been mind-blowing, and I guess I'm still processing and taking my anger out on you. It's not fair, and I'm sorry."

"It's okay, Ty. Everyone has a bad day once in a while. But full disclosure, I'm going to have Sebastian take a look at these papers. I want to be very sure they are real, and I want to know who sent them. Because whoever it was, they are just trying to start trouble. Or they're trying to scam us out of something. Not today, Satan. Not today."

That got him to crack a smile.

"I'll handle it from here. Do you trust me?"

"Always, despite the momentary lapse in judgment," Ty said.

"Good to hear," I said, chuckling. "We'll get to the bottom of it."

"I love you, Mama Marion."

I grinned at him. "Love you, too."

As I watched him leave the house and head to the garage apartment, I focused on the duplicate papers and definitely felt something cold and slimy in the pit of my stomach. It was a sign that I was on to something. These papers hadn't just shown up. Someone was knee-deep in Ty's business, and I was going to track them down because it was clear to me that Carson and whoever he was working with were after more than a family connection.

It always, *always* seemed to come down to money and greed.

This situation was no exception.

CHAPTER 22

I sat in the passenger seat, frustrated that I was on my way to see Trace Foster when what I really wanted to do was find Carson and confront him. I was fairly positive he was working at Sky's the Limit, which meant all I had to do was drive downtown to get my answers. Surely, I could use my powers of persuasion to at least get a modicum of information out of the guy.

Since he'd arrived in Premonition Pointe, everything had gone south, and now with the new trust paperwork, I was certain he was at the heart of everything.

"I don't want to stay long," I told Charlotte, who was in the back seat. Jax was driving, as he had done ever since he'd been bitten by the wolf. It was as if he couldn't go anywhere unless he had his hands on the wheel. And while he'd always been inclined to drive before, he hadn't been quite so militant about it.

On one hand, his alpha energy was pretty damned hot, especially in the bedroom. But in day-to day-life, I suspected it was going to get annoying quickly. I'd always been a little too independent for my own good. I just hoped we'd find some sort of happy medium.

My phone buzzed, indicating I had a voice mail. I frowned at my phone, wondering why I hadn't heard it ring. I pressed play and bit back a wince when Hollister's voice said, "I'm sorry it's taken so long for me to call you back, Marion," over the SUV's stereo system. After Jax's unusual display of jealousy when it came to the man, this was going to be awkward.

Jax cut his narrowed eyes to me. "You were waiting on Hollister to call you back?"

I shushed him so that I could hear what the other man had to say.

"I've read every publication I could get my hands on about the werewolf curse," the messaged continued. "The consensus is that there is no cure."

"Whatever," Jax said, maintaining the same attitude he'd had since the day he left the hospital. He felt fine and said, if anything, he had more energy. He hadn't shifted or lost control and torn anyone apart, so in his mind, there really wasn't anything to worry about. If only I'd had his confidence.

"But there is an elixir that most shifters take so that they can control their shifting," Hollister was saying. His signal must have cut out, and it was difficult to understand the next line. When it cleared, he was saying something about cookies. "Without them, the wolves wouldn't be able to control their shifting during the full moon. Give me a call, and I'll explain it more in detail. Say hi to Charlotte."

"Hi, Hollister," Charlotte sang from the back seat.

"Good luck to Jax."

"I don't need any luck," Jax mumbled, making me roll my eyes.

The message ended, and I sat back in my seat. "That's a relief."

"What is?" Jax asked.

"That there's an elixir to help control the shift. That's great news, right?"

"Sure. I don't know where we get this elixir or if that's even something I need though. It's not like I've wolfed out or anything."

That was true. He hadn't. Last night had been a full moon, and while he'd been agitated, he hadn't shifted. Was shifting during a full moon even a thing, or was that just an urban legend? So far, Jax's only shift had been his dominating demeanor. I supposed that was something I could talk to Hollister about when I didn't have shoddy cell service.

"Take a left just after this red barn," Charlotte said from the back seat.

"I know," Jax shot back. We were on a country road, out in the rural part of Premonition Pointe on the east side, miles away from the ocean. There wasn't much around except a whole lot of trees and homesteads every two or three miles.

"Just making sure, wolf boy," she said just to irritate him. She'd bestowed the nickname on him the day before after declaring his alpha energy was getting on her last nerve.

"That's it on the right. The small blue one with all the outbuildings," Charlotte said.

Jax didn't stop.

"Hey, I said that was it." She leaned forward between the seats and added, "I thought you knew where you were going."

"I do," he said flatly and then pulled the SUV off to the side of the road behind a stand of large trees.

"Nicely done," I said when I realized the SUV would be hidden from the road. There was no point in calling attention to ourselves out here in the woods. We didn't know exactly what we'd be walking in on.

I jumped out of the car and grabbed my dagger, feeling more confident when my fingers wrapped around the hilt. For the past couple of days, I'd been filled with anxiety from all the uncertainty in my life. But when I had that metal handle in my hand and felt the magic pulsating just beneath my fingertips, I always felt like I could take on the weight of the world and come out victorious.

It was a tremendous confidence boost.

Jax took the lead, heading across the street into the woods. Charlotte and I glanced at each other briefly before taking off after him.

"If I'd known we were going to rough it, I'd have worn different shoes," Charlotte complained.

I glanced down and spotted her hot pink sparkly wedges. They weren't the worst shoe in the world to be traipsing around the woods in, but they were close. "Char," I whispered with a shake of my head. "Really?"

"What? How was I supposed to know it was going to be a recon mission? I was just planning to knock on his front door. You know, the way normal people go about things when they just want some simple information."

Jax circled back and pressed his finger to his lips, indicating that it was time to be quiet.

Charlotte and I fell in step behind him, trusting that he had a plan. It was one we hadn't discussed, but he seemed so sure of himself it was hard not to follow.

Alpha energy.

The words floated through my mind, and I couldn't disagree.

Jax came to a stop and moved behind a tree, indicating for us to stay close behind him. It all felt very 007 if you asked me. I was in Charlotte's camp. I'd have just walked up to the front door and started asking the guy questions. But if Jax had some intuition that we should do it this way, then it couldn't hurt, could it?

Famous last words, I told myself as we darted from tree to tree. Out in the country, sometimes it was shoot first and ask questions later. I gripped the dagger tighter and prayed Jax knew what he was doing.

"There," Jax whispered as he pointed toward two small cabins in a clearing.

I peered between the trees and spotted Trace Foster sitting on the porch of the closest cabin. He was wearing only ripped jeans and nothing else. "Now what?" I asked. "It's going to look really suspicious if we just pop out of the woods."

Trace's head jerked up, and he held perfectly still as he seemed to listen for something.

For us? Had he heard me? We weren't that close, but out in the stillness of the country, sometimes voices did carry.

"Marion?" Charlotte said, clutching my hand.

Immediately, my stomach roiled and my head started to ache.

"Charlotte?" I turned and spotted her green face. She looked weak and like she was going to pass out.

"It's that same... energy. From the office. Only it's—" She fell to her knees and retched.

Trace Foster jumped off his porch and ran flat out toward us.

"Shit," I muttered and tried to help Charlotte to her feet. When she could barely move, I pressed the dagger into her hand and wrapped her fingers around the hilt. Finally, she was able to get to her feet, though her green coloring remained.

"Go back to the car," Jax ordered.

"No." Charlotte was defiant. "That's who broke into our office. I want to know why."

I blinked at my sister. She sounded fiercer than I'd ever heard her before. "How can you be sure it was him?"

"I'd recognize that energy anywhere," she said through gritted teeth.

I frowned, still not sure what to do. Hadn't Charlotte met him once before at the mixer when Sara had chosen her dates? Or was that the night she'd left early for her own date? I knew at least one of Sara's picks had arrived later. Had it been Trace?

"Char," I asked her quickly, "have you ever seen that guy before?"

She shook her head and nearly lost her lunch again, but she managed to hold it together this time.

Okay, that explained a few things at least.

When Trace was about ten feet away, Jax walked out of the woods to meet him.

The other man stopped in his tracks when he spotted Jax. "This is private property," he growled. "I suggest you leave before that's no longer an option."

"Not until I get some questions answered," Jax said, folding his arms over his chest.

"You're not going to get any answers here." Trace nodded toward the woods. "I suggest you go back to wherever you came from."

"I think it might be a little too late for that, don't you?" Jax reached back behind his neck and quickly tugged his shirt over his head. Twisting to the side, he bent his head, showing off the impressive mark and purple spiderweb of lines that had been left by the wolf bite. "Who exactly do I have to thank for this?"

The other man shrugged, portraying disinterest. "How would I know?"

"Because you have the same parting gift."

He did? I peered through the trees, trying to see the man's curse, but all I saw was a fit man who bore the scar of an animal attack across his chest. Bear? Some sort of large cat? There were four slashes in a row where he'd been swiped. They'd healed long ago.

Trace bristled. "How do you know that?"

"I can smell it."

"What do you want?" Trace growled. "Why are you here?"

"We're here for answers," Jax said. He waved at me and Charlotte, indicating that we should come out of the trees.

"I don't know anything." Trace turned and started walking back toward the cabin.

"Why did you break into my office?" I called out. "What were you looking for?"

He stopped in his tracks and turned to look at me. "Marion Matched. You think I broke into your office? After that crazy bitch you set me up with tried to kill me, why would I ever come near you again?"

"That's what I want to know," I said, standing there with my fists clenched and radiating with anger. "You hacked my files. Why?"

He snorted. "Pure fiction. Get the hell out of here before I call the cops."

"Marion Matched," a deeper voice said with a low chuckle.

I spun to the left and spotted a man who looked vaguely familiar. He was tall with salt-and-pepper hair, wide shoulders, and a slightly crooked nose. But it was the self-satisfied smile that I recognized. He was someone I'd known a long time ago. What was his name?

Phil? Parker? Pacey?

No, it was Phineas. Phineas Davies. He'd worked at the drive-in theater in our hometown, and Trish had harbored a massive crush on the guy.

"Phineas. What brings you to Premonition Pointe?"

"Family business." He rubbed at his jawline and appeared to study her. "You seem to be having some trouble these days."

"Nothing I can't handle," I said coolly.

"What about you?" he asked Jax, his dark eyes blazing

with challenge. "Looks like you got into a fight with a wolf and lost."

Jax stared him down, unmoved by his taunting. "I imagine if I'd truly lost, I'd have been dead by now."

The hair on the back of my neck stood up. The tension between Jax and Phineas was so thick it was hard to even breathe. What was going on? Did they know each other? "Jax? What is happening?"

"Phineas over there tried to kill me." He tapped the bite on his neck. "This bite was courtesy of him and his pack."

I sucked in a sharp breath. "How do you know that?"

"It's the pack connection," Phineas said with a shit-eating grin. "I'm his maker. He's compelled to do whatever I say. Isn't that convenient?"

"You think so?" Jax asked, sounding bored.

"I don't just think so. I know so," Phineas snarled. "If I tell you to sit down and lick your balls, you'll do it. Understand?"

Jax actually chuckled.

Trace glanced between Phineas and Jax, his eyes shifting as if he were just waiting for some sort of signal.

Phineas's face turned a dark shade of maroon as anger seemed to crawl up his neck. "You dare defy me?"

"You're nothing to me except a piece of shit who tried to intimidate a friend of mine to keep her from getting in your way. You don't own me like you do this one." Jax waved an impatient hand toward Trace. "You might have cursed him to do your bidding, but you'll never have me."

What in the hell was Jax talking about? How did he know anything about Trace and Phineas, and why did Phineas think Jax would do his bidding? Was it an alpha thing? Phineas bit Jax and seemed to be under the impression that Jax would be under his spell or something.

"On your knees, wolf!" Phineas ordered Jax.

Jax raised one eyebrow. "Looks like things aren't going according to your plan, Phineas. Now what are you going to do?"

Phineas let out a loud howl and then tore his clothes off as he fell to the ground, his body twisting and contorting as he shifted into the large white and gray wolf I'd seen that day in the cave. Magic crackled through the air, and suddenly Trace's back arched and he also fell and quickly shifted into a smaller, leaner gray wolf.

Charlotte sucked in a gasp. "Whoa," she said. "I don't feel that energy when he's in wolf form."

"Was Trace there that day at the beach? Was he one of the three guys who threatened you?"

She shook her head and then screamed, "Jax! Look out!"

CHAPTER 23

J turned around just in time to see Phineas lunge at Jax with his teeth bared. Without even thinking, I grabbed the dagger from Charlotte and stepped forward to slash at the wolf, but he flew past me and landed on Jax, taking him down.

"No!" I cried and started to try again. But just as I raised my arm again, the other wolf hit me from behind, knocking me flat on my face. "Oomph!" I said into the dirt.

"Move, Marion!" Charlotte called.

I rolled and came up swinging. This time I did connect with the wolf but barely, just leaving a small slash mark on his hind leg. The wolf yelped and leaped away, only to come right back, growling as drool dripped from his jowls.

"Stay away from my sister!" Charlotte cried, waving her hands at the wolf as if that would scare him off.

He turned his attention on her and leaped, going straight for her throat.

"No!" I jumped in between them and sank the dagger

right into his left shoulder. The wolf fell to the ground with the dagger still lodged in his flesh. Charlotte and I both went for it at the same time, and when our hands touched, magic shot from the dagger, engulfing the wolf. A second later, he was lying naked on the ground in his human form.

Charlotte and I stared at each other, both of us still holding the dagger.

But then a howl behind us made us both turn to find Jax and Phineas locked in a vicious fight. Phineas was on top of Jax, his jaws locked on Jax's upraised forearm. Every muscle in Jax's body was strained as he worked to fight off the wolf.

My heart began to race, and my chest constricted as air refused to move through my lungs. I felt as if I was watching my life slip away from me in slow motion, and there was little or nothing I could do about it.

"Marion! Move!" Charlotte cried and tugged on my arm.

When I saw that Jax's arm was shaking and that sweat was pouring off his face, I knew he was struggling. He'd lose this battle with Phineas, and then what would happen? Would the wolf tear him apart?

That thought finally propelled me forward. Charlotte and I were just about to attack Phineas when another wolf came out of nowhere and ran straight toward us. But instead of trying to bite either of us, the wolf rolled right at our feet, knocking us both down.

"Hurry," I ordered Charlotte as I watched Phineas tear a chunk of skin right off Jax's arm.

My sister got to her feet but stumbled just before she reached me.

Jax was staring wide-eyed up at the wolf who was

snarling down at him. The wolf raised his head, howled, and then dove for Jax's jugular.

"No!" I screamed just as a smaller, dark gray wolf appeared out of nowhere and knocked Phineas off Jax. The two wolves rolled over and over as they tore into each other's flesh. Fur and blood flew from the pair as they tried to kill each other.

I ran over to Jax, who'd already found his shirt and was using it as a bandage for his injured arm. "We have to get out of here," I said and tugged him to his feet. "Let's get Charlotte and—"

"No, Marion. Not yet. I still need answers," he said, shaking his head at me.

"What?" I asked, horrified. "That wolf almost killed you."

"That wolf created me," he said gently. "I need to know what happens next."

My heart sank. "I get that you need answers, but don't you think it's too dangerous right now? We don't know how many other wolves are here. Hell, Jax, we walked into a literal den of wolves. It's not safe for us here."

"It's not safe for you and Charlotte," he corrected me. "You both should go. Get back to the SUV. I'll find a way back."

"Hell no!" I shouted and wanted to throttle him. "What in the devil's lettuce makes you think I'd leave you here, of all places, and just run back home, Jax Williams? What kind of person do you think I am?"

"The kind who isn't a werewolf. And I'd like to keep it that way. Please, Marion. Do this for me."

"No," I said without even thinking about it. "I will not leave you here on your own."

"It's a good thing you don't have to," an eerily familiar voice said from right behind me.

I spun, unable to believe my ears. But then I saw her face and just stared at her in stunned silence.

"Marion?" Trish Kirkwood asked tentatively. "I didn't give you a stroke, did I?"

"Trish?" I asked, unable to believe my eyes. Surely I was hallucinating. Trish had died five years ago. She couldn't be here now. This had to be some sort of psychotic break due to all the stress, right?

"Hi, Marion." She gave me a whisper of a smile.

I scanned her robe-clad body and then quickly glanced around to find Phineas was lying on the ground, back in his human form. Another woman I'd never seen before was kneeling near him, zip-tying his feet together. Charlotte was busy tying Trace's hands behind his back. The man was lying on his side, still knocked out from the stab wound and the magic we'd poured into him.

"Charlotte?" I called. "Are you okay?"

My sister turned to look at me and nodded sharply. "I don't feel that energy anymore. I think we killed it when we poured magic into him."

"That's good," I said and then scanned the area for Jax. He was sitting near Phineas, watching the woman secure him in case he came to.

"I'm sure you have a lot of questions for me," Trish said, sounding nervous.

"I do, but…" Shaking my head, I stepped forward and wrapped my friend in my arms, holding her tightly. "Holy hell, Trish. I missed you more than you know."

Trish wrapped her arms around me, holding on tightly.

It wasn't until she started to shake slightly in my arms that I realized she was crying. When she spoke, her words were barely audible through her sobs. "I've missed you so much."

Sorrow, frustration, and pure anger rushed through me, and I had to take a step back to get ahold of myself. "Where the fuck have you been?"

Oops. That probably wasn't the best way to start that conversation.

"I was... around, but—"

"*Around*," I screamed. "Around what? Certainly not your son. Oh, I mean *sons*. Thanks for omitting that little tidbit of information. It sure would have been nice to know that Ty had a brother all these years."

Trish winced. "Okay, I guess I deserve that. But I really do have a good explanation if you'll just let me finish."

"First, explain this." I waved a hand at her robe. "Why are you dressed like you're working in a brothel?"

"You'd rather I just walked around naked?" she asked, her eyebrows raised.

"What? No... oh shit," I said softly. "No." I shook my head, trying to dislodge my crazy thoughts. But then I couldn't let it go. I had to know. "Trish, are you a werewolf?"

Her smile vanished as she pursed her lips together. "Who else could've taken down Phineas other than me?" Trish wrapped her arms around herself and watched as her friend kept an eye on Phineas until... Until what?

"Are you?" I asked again.

She gave me a slow nod.

"How long?" I demanded.

"It's been five years," she said, holding my gaze. "Five

years since I walked out on Ty, you, and everyone else in my life."

"Did you leave for our benefit or for your own?" I asked, not bothering to keep the judgment out of my tone. I knew in my heart she must've left to keep her loved ones safe, but that didn't mean I wasn't still furious.

"Both," she admitted. "I'm not going to lie, Marion, it was the worst days of my life right after Phineas bit me. I thought I was going to die. And then the shift came, and I knew I had to leave. For all our sakes."

"And you're back now. Why?" I couldn't help asking the question.

"For you. For Ty and Carson. And for Jax." She glanced over her shoulder at my boyfriend, who was sitting near Phineas. "He's going to need a pack, and if I'd let Phineas get to him…" She gave an involuntary shudder. "Let's just say I'm the lesser of two evils."

"You're not evil," I said automatically.

"You don't know that, Marion," she said. "You haven't seen the things I have."

I blinked at her. "Like what?"

She just shook her head. "Come on. Let's go. We have a werewolf to interrogate."

I stared at Trish's muscular frame as she moved to stand next to Phineas.

And that's when it hit me like a ton of bricks. The jawline, the nose, the dark hair. But most of all, their frames were all but identical.

Phineas was Carson's dad.

CHAPTER 24

I heard a rustling in the trees, and I clutched the dagger and reached for Charlotte's hand. "Someone is coming," I whispered.

I was still shaken by Trish's sudden appearance, and I didn't recognize the man right off when he stomped out of the woods holding a handgun trained right at Trish.

"Step away from him," the man ordered, his voice vaguely familiar.

My eyes jerked up and pure rage thrummed through me when I recognized him.

It was Andrew, Sara's lawyer. And right behind him was the nerdy science guy, and he was clutching a crossbow.

"Holy shit. What's happening right now?" Charlotte whispered to me.

"I don't know." I glanced over at Jax, who was tracking the two men, his lips twisted into a snarl.

Trish and her friend both stood slowly with their hands in the air.

"Andrew," Trish said coolly. "I wondered when you'd show up."

"You should have listened when Phineas told you to leave and never come back," Andrew shot back at her. "Now, instead of you getting to enjoy a nice life off the grid in the woods, I'm going to bury you in them."

Her eyes narrowed and pure hatred seemed to radiate from her. "I'd like to see you try."

Without warning, Andrew fired a shot, hitting her in her left thigh.

"Trish!" I cried as she fell to one knee, snarling at the supposed lawyer. I'd had a feeling he was bad news, but I'd never imagined he was this terrible.

"You're going to pay for that," Trish barked out, clutching her bleeding leg.

"That's what you always say, and yet, here I am. But I'm not worried because once Phineas is free, he'll take care of you. I told him not to leave loose ends." Andrew and his minion barely glanced at us as he stalked toward Trish. "I always told him his worst mistake was sleeping with you."

"Funny," she said with a sarcastic tilt of her head. "I told him the same thing about you."

"You fucking bitch." He raised the gun again, but before he could get the shot off, I lunged, aiming for his chest. He dropped the gun and grabbed my wrist, squeezing so tightly I lost control of the dagger. It skittered into the brush as the two of us clawed at each other.

My self-defense training kicked in and I went for his eyes first, jabbing his left one with my thumb. When he let out a howl of pain, I brought my knee up with as much force as I could muster. But when my knee only hit air, I looked up to see Jax holding the guy by the throat, threatening to rip his head off.

Andrew's face turned bright red, and I started to wonder if his head was going to explode. Andrew kicked out, catching Jax in the chest, making them both crash to the ground. I searched frantically for the gun or my dagger, desperate to help Jax.

"Marion! Watch out!" Charlotte cried just as a bolt whizzed by my head.

I rolled and came up crouching on my feet just in time to see Andrew's sidekick aim the crossbow at me again. But before he could get the shot off, a loud bang filled the air and he fell forward, landing right in front of me. A bloom of blood pooled on his back as his eyes stared blankly at nothing.

"Marion?" Brix Erikson said, standing over me with a worried expression. "Are you all right?"

"Brix?" I stared up at him, wondering if I was hallucinating. "Is that really you?"

He reached down and held out a hand to me, hauling me to my feet.

"I thought you were working undercover," I said, glancing around for Jax. He'd gotten the best of Andrew and was now holding him down despite his wounded arm, making sure he didn't cause any more trouble while Trish struggled to tie him up. Her friend arrived at her side, helping her and Jax get him under control.

"I was." He waved a hand at the compound. "I was busy following a criminal wolf pack that was engaging in every crime known to man when Trish got word to me that you'd been targeted. If I hadn't been completely off grid, I'd have been here sooner."

"You know Trish?" I turned to study her, my head spinning with questions. "You were undercover with her to bust Phineas?"

He shook his head. "No. I was dealing with a different pack. Trish just knew how to get word to me that there was trouble. I know you have a lot of questions. But right now, both Jax and Trish need medical attention, and I need to get this situation cleaned up before my cover is blown." He glanced at Trish. "You'd better go get that leg fixed, and I'll check in with you later."

Trish nodded at him. Then she started hobbling over to me with the help of her friend. I met her halfway, and she placed a hand on my cheek as she said, "I'll be in touch."

I watched as they moved slowly toward the trees and then disappeared.

"Holy shit. This is insane," Charlotte said, staring at the gory scene in front of us in awe.

"You can say that again." I walked over to Jax. "Come on. Let's go."

"Not until I have answers," he said, his face contorted in pain. Then he turned to Brix. "Why haven't I shifted?"

Brix glanced up at him thoughtfully. "You didn't shift last night during the full moon?"

"No."

"Did you have the urge to shift?" Brix asked.

"No. But I felt like I was turning into someone—or some*thing*—else while I was fighting that wolf today. But I was still just me."

"Interesting." Brix studied him for a long moment. "It's

either one of two things. It's possible someone gave you a dose of the elixir that keeps you from shifting. Or you could have been magically bound, and while you'll have all the traits of a wolf, you won't be able to shift."

My heart pounded against my ribcage. Magically bound? Was it possible that the magic Charlotte and I had used to heal his wound had saved him from becoming a full-fledged werewolf?

Jax's eyes met mine, and I knew he was wondering the same thing.

"Well, this just got really interesting," Charlotte said.

Brix's phone buzzed. He glanced at it and then at us. "You should go. I'll be in touch later tonight."

I knew better than to ask exactly why he needed us to leave. Brix was the director of the Magical Task Force, and he held a lot of secrets close to the vest. If he was still trying to protect his undercover operation, he didn't need us blowing his cover.

I nodded to Charlotte. "Come on."

"But what about Trace? We never did get our answers." She walked over to where the man was still lying on the ground, naked. "Who poisoned everyone?"

He stared up at her, and just when I thought he wasn't going to respond, he said, "I did. For Phineas. It was his plan all along. It was the curse. I had no choice in the matter." Then his eyes rolled into the back of his head, and his body convulsed.

Nausea overtook me as I watched Trace's mouth foam, and then suddenly, he was completely still, staring blankly at nothing.

"Shit," Brix said, moving to stand over Trace. "That piece

of shit Phineas cursed one of his own." He glanced at me. "Did you break it?"

"The curse?" I asked.

He nodded. "Wolves are compelled to do their sire's bidding, but it's not always that cut-and-dried. Some are strong enough to break that bond. When that happens, they are either kicked out of the pack or cursed with dark magic. If that curse is broken, it often kills the wolf."

"The curse was broken," Charlotte confirmed. "I could feel it when I was around his energy, but when Marion and I stabbed him, it disappeared. The energy was gone."

"We killed him?" I asked with a gasp.

"No, the curse did." Brix let out a long, tired sigh. "Okay. Go. Now. Don't whisper even a word of this to anyone. There's a reason no one ever talks about werewolves. Tell the healer you find for Jax that his wound was a dog attack."

It took everything in me to put one foot in front of the other and not ask a million more questions, but I knew Brix was true to his word. If he said he'd be in touch, then he would. The only thing left to do was to get Jax to a healer.

CHAPTER 25

There wasn't much the healer could do for Jax. She cleaned the wound with herbs, gave him a pain potion, and told him to keep the wound dry for a couple of weeks. Then she sent us on our way.

No one said anything on the way back to town. Too much had happened. We all had too many questions and not enough answers. My head was spinning. Phineas and Andrew were lovers? Phineas was Carson's dad? Was Carson a part of their criminal wolf pack?

I quickly texted Ty and told him that I needed him to avoid Carson until we were able to talk. That it was important.

The text that came back made my heart sink. *He's my brother. I'm not going to ignore him. And if this is about the trust, it doesn't matter. He deserves his share.*

Instead of playing the text game, I hit Ty's number and willed him to pick up. The call went straight to voice mail.

"Dammit." I sent another text indicating it wasn't about

the money and that I'd explain when I got home, but my text went unanswered.

Despite his bandaged arm, Jax was still driving. It was like a new compulsion for the man. Charlotte and I had both insisted that he should take a breather and let one of us drive, but he wasn't having it.

It wasn't long before he pulled up in front of Sebastian and Gigi's big white house that sat along the shoreline. Earlier in the day, Sebastian had asked us to meet him there instead of at his office, which was perfectly fine with me. The less people we ran into the better as far as I was concerned. After the day we'd had, we all needed a shower and a change of clothes.

Gigi opened the door before we even rang the doorbell. "Where the hell have you guys been? We expected you hours ago, and we've been worried." She scanned our appearance and raised both eyebrows. "Did you participate in a pig wrestling contest?"

"Close. It was wolves," I said and walked into the house. I didn't stop in the living room. I was afraid I'd dirty up her pristine white furnishings, so I kept right on going until I led everyone out to the patio. The waves churned against the rocks while the late afternoon sun sparkled off the brilliant blue sea. "I'd never leave this patio if I lived here," I said, sitting on a resin chair.

"It is tough sometimes," Gigi admitted. "I'm going to go get drinks and let Sebastian know you're here. Any preferences?"

We all asked for water and then sat in silence until Sebastian walked out carrying a file.

I glanced up at him, taking in his neat short-sleeved

button-down shirt and slate gray slacks. He looked like money, while we looked like hobos who'd just walked off a boxcar after riding the rails.

Sebastian took a long look at us. "Looks like you ran into trouble today."

"You can say that again." I started to launch into the story but then remembered that Brix didn't want us to say anything about the wolves, so I used wording I knew Sebastian would understand. "Let's just say it was Magical Task Force business. I'm not really allowed to say anything. I can tell you that I think Sara's case is going to be dropped shortly."

He raised one eyebrow. "Really? Interesting. That's not surprising since Trace Foster's online footprint has mostly been erased. There are records of him, but most everything about him has been cleaned up to make it look like he's just a regular guy. In reality, he has a record for larceny, theft, and a bunch of break-ins. It wreaks of a professional digital sweep. That's why you didn't find anything on him."

"What? I need to stop using that service for background checks. I'm only going through you now," I vowed.

Sebastian nodded. "Please do. Also Andrew Miller doesn't have a digital footprint prior to six months ago."

"He doesn't?" I asked. "No records anywhere?"

"None whatsoever. That usually means a person has assumed a new identity."

"What about witness protection?" Charlotte asked. "I hear those people don't have a traceable path either."

"Doubtful. The powers that be at least make an effort to give them a past with birth records and traces of old jobs or addresses even if they are fake. Whoever made up Andrew's past didn't even try. There's no actual record of his attorney's license or a trail of addresses or even a driver's license in any of the states. Unless he came from another country, that would be virtually impossible."

"What if they'd been living off grid?" Jax asked, leaning forward.

"That's a possibility for sure. Like if they were in a cult or something. But there would still likely be some records somewhere in the system. Even people who go off grid usually haven't spent their entire lives away from civilization."

"Unless they were born into a cult," Charlotte mused. "I knew a guy like that. Biggest freak you've ever met. I mean, if one was looking for someone to heat up the sheets—"

I cleared my throat. "Thanks for that, Charlotte."

She grinned at me, a sign she was starting to feel a little more like herself after the confrontation in the woods.

Sebastian chuckled. "She's not wrong though. Cult members are notoriously hard to track. But this doesn't feel like that. I think these are assumed identities. Which means this is a scam." He opened a folder. "These are the files that were hacked in your system."

I scanned the paperwork. It included my personal files that contained Trish's will and the trust for Ty. And my most recent clients' files had been scanned, which gave the hackers enough information that they'd be able to track down almost anything they wanted about the person, including banking information. The realization made me feel sick.

"You'll see that Sara's has been highlighted," Sebastian said.

I took another look and sure enough, they'd flagged that file. "Why?"

"Because when we looked deeper, it appears your client is sitting on a load of assets. Her land alone is worth millions. Plus, there are other investments. If anyone wanted to target a single woman, she'd be the kind of cash cow they were looking for."

"Makes sense," I said. "It's the only thing that adds up, right? Trace poisoned the men so that Andrew could act as her lawyer and bilk her for money. Or worse. It was a perfect trap. Become friends with her through Facebook to gain her trust and then pounce once the trap had been set."

"I don't understand," Charlotte said. "Didn't Sara say she'd been friends with Andrew for months? If he knew she was a cash cow already, why did he have to hack our files?"

"Likely to get information he didn't have like bank account numbers or a social security number since Marion collects that to do her background checks," Sebastian said. "He might have known she had assets, but he needed to know where to look for them."

"Seems like a lot of work for farmland," Charlotte said.

I chuckled. "Farmland on the coast is worth millions if it's more than a few acres."

"Sara Groveland owns over a *hundred* acres," Sebastian said.

"Shit." Charlotte's eyes looked like they were going to pop out of her head. "So that explains a lot."

"A lot, but not everything," I said, thinking about Carson. "What about Carson? Did you do a check on him?"

Sebastian pressed his lips together into a thin line as he nodded. "His past is a little different. There's not much of anything on him for the past five years except for the fact that there's a credit lock on his name. It feels like he was trying to protect himself from identity theft. But before that, I did find adoption records, school records, a graduation photo. There's not much to go on, but he's real, and he's definitely Trish's son."

That was a relief. Right? It meant he hadn't been lying at least. "I think maybe Ty's brother is trying to scam him." I quickly explained the second trust that had shown up in the mailbox.

Sebastian frowned, his dark eyes looking stormy. "Get me that paperwork. I'll vet it and we'll go from there. Whatever you do, don't let Ty sign anything."

"I already told him that's what we'd do." I stood. "Thanks for everything, Sebastian. You've helped clear a few things up. I'll get that paperwork to you as soon as possible."

We said our goodbyes and then went home, showered, and the three of us just waited.

And waited.

And waited some more.

Finally, just before ten o'clock, Ty walked in.

I jumped up from the couch and ran over to him, inspecting him as if he'd been away for months. "Where have you been?"

He frowned at me. "I was at work, and then I was out looking for Carson. Kennedy said he left work sick today, so I was worried about him. But he wasn't at his apartment or anywhere else in town. I even checked with the hospital just in case he checked himself in. No luck."

"He's just missing?"

"I wouldn't say that." Trish's quiet voice came from the back door, making me jump.

I whirled around. "Trish, what the fuck? Where have you been all day? Never mind that, where the hell have you been for the past five years?"

"Mom?" Ty gasped out.

I spun around, finding the man I thought of as a son standing there with his hand over his mouth and his face as white as a sheet. His eyes flickered to me. "Is my mom standing at the back door, or am I hallucinating?"

"Ty," Trish said, her tone anguished.

He looked at her and then back at me. "Marion?"

"It's her. This is what I wanted to talk to you about, Ty. She just—"

"You're alive!" Ty flew to her, grabbing her up in a hug and lifting her right off the ground. When he put her back down, she winced, and it was then that I saw the bandage wrapped around her leg. I supposed shifting didn't fix bullet holes. Ty glanced down at her leg and asked, "What happened?"

"It's a long story," she said, cupping her palm to his cheek. "I've missed you, baby."

Ty's joy suddenly disappeared and was replaced by pure confusion as his brow furrowed and he frowned at her. "Where the hell have you been? How is it you're not dead?" Then the anger flared to life. "You were alive this entire time, and you just let me think you were dead?"

"She had a good reason," Carson said, stepping through the back door and reaching for Trish's hand.

Trish held on tightly to her eldest son as she stared at Ty

with anguish and regret in her eyes. "I'm so sorry, Ty. I did what I thought would keep you safe."

Ty shook his head. "This isn't happening. My own mother did not fake her death and leave me all alone only to walk back into my life with a brother I'd never known about." He walked over to stand next to me. "Did you know about this?"

The pain and accusation in his tone nearly broke me. "No," I said, staring him in the eye. "That isn't something I'd ever keep from you."

Trish let out a quiet, anguished cry. "I didn't have a choice."

"There's always a choice," Ty said, shooting daggers at her with his eyes. "Whatever the reason, it was cruel."

"Please, Ty. Won't you just hear me out? I'll explain everything," she begged.

Ty sucked in a sharp breath. He walked into my bedroom, leaving all of us wondering what he was doing. But when he returned a moment later, he had a fist full of paperwork. The paperwork I'd left on my desk. "First, tell me one thing. Is this real?"

Both Trish and Carson frowned.

"What is that?" Carson asked.

"A trust that says you're entitled to half of what Mom left me. Did you leave it in my mailbox?"

The two glanced at each other, both appearing confused. Finally, Carson said, "No. Why would I do that? I have my own trust."

Trish limped forward and took the paperwork, scanned it, and then scowled. "Phineas did this." She pointed to a space on the bottom with an address for a lawyer. "That's his go-to office space for his scams."

"That piece of shit," Carson said with disgust, the kind that lingers in the air. "I wish you'd have killed him today." He said it with such conviction that I fully believed it was how he felt.

Ty stared at them. "Phineas? I think someone needs to fill me in. Who's that?"

Carson turned his repulsed gaze on his half brother. "My father. He's the reason Mom faked her death five years ago."

CHAPTER 26

*W*e moved outside to my backyard and gathered around the small fire pit, waiting for Trish to explain herself. Ty sat between me and Jax with Charlotte on my other side. Trish and Carson were directly across from Ty.

"There's a lot that I shielded you from, Ty," Trish said. "I thought I was protecting you. That's my only excuse."

Ty stared at her, seemingly immune to her obvious pain. "I don't want excuses. I just want an explanation."

"That's fair," Trish said, flicking her gaze to me.

"I'm with Ty," I said, realizing for the first time that maybe I hadn't ever really known my best friend. "You didn't even tell me about Carson. I have to say, that was quite a shock."

"I didn't tell anyone," she said quietly. "It wasn't long after I found out I was pregnant that I realized something about Phineas wasn't right. I don't know exactly how, but I knew he was dangerous. And when I found out he was a high-level scam artist, I did everything in my power to make sure he didn't know about Carson. That's why I never said anything when I went away to school and then gave him up. I never wanted Phineas to have contact with him."

"Obviously, that failed," I said and turned to Carson. "How long have you known your father?"

"Since I was seventeen," he said with obvious disgust dripping from his tone. "My parents were killed, and then he pretended to be my uncle and took me in. I didn't know at the time that he was the one who killed them."

Both Ty and I let out a shocked gasp. Jax remained silent, taking it all in.

"So that entire story you told me about your adoptive mother dying and you being raised by your father on the farm was a complete fabrication?" Ty asked him, unable to hide his frustration.

Carson averted his gaze. "Yes. It's the story I tell so that I don't have to talk about my parents being murdered."

Ty nodded once, indicating he understood. If all this was true, Carson's history was tragic. I could see why he'd fabricate something new.

"That's when I went after him," Trish said. "I kept in touch with Carson's adoptive parents. It was sort of like an open adoption. I'd known them for years, and when they went missing, I found out from their neighbor that an uncle had shown up to take Carson. He didn't have any uncles. That's when I found out Phineas had known about Carson the entire time. He'd just been waiting until Carson was old enough to join his gang of trashy criminals. It took me a long time to track them down, and when I did, I stumbled onto the knowledge that they were werewolves. I knew then that I had to get him out before they turned him, too."

"So, werewolves are made, not born?" Jax asked and then flicked his gaze to me. The intent of the question couldn't be clearer. If he were to get me pregnant—although highly unlikely at my age—would the baby be human or werewolf?

"They are definitely made. Only the bite of a wolf can infect someone with the werewolf curse," Trish confirmed.

Jax nodded.

"It took me over five years to devise a plan to free Carson, but I finally did and set him up with a trust so that he never needed to rely on anyone. But the night I freed him and we were ready to flee, Phineas came after me. He wanted Carson's location, but I wouldn't give it to him. In the end, we made a deal. He'd leave Carson and Ty alone if I joined his pack. I knew then that if I said no, he'd just kill me and go after Carson anyway. He's not a good person. So I sacrificed myself. Carson got a new life, and I had a criminal's word he'd leave my sons alone."

"Looks like that didn't work out, did it?" Charlotte said, voicing the thought no one else wanted to say.

"It worked for a while. I faked my death, joined his pack, and did my level best to destroy everything he tried to do to scam people. I was careful, always keeping an eye on Ty and Marion, making sure they were safe. Phineas never bothered them. I figured he was holding up his end of the deal. But eventually, he threw me out of the pack, which was fine with me. I became an informant for the Magical Task Force, and that's when he showed up here, going after the people I love the most." She looked at me and Ty. "Both of you and, of course, anyone else he could scam out of money."

"But not Carson?" I asked, still skeptical.

"No. He didn't even know where he was. When I told Carson what was going on, he insisted on coming here and keeping an eye on all of you. He knows how awful Phineas is and didn't want anyone to get hurt."

"Those cookies he brought Jax in the hospital," I said. "Did they have the werewolf suppressing elixir in them?"

She nodded and turned to Jax. "I didn't want you to shift until you had someone there to help you through it. The cookies keep the wolf suppressed."

"Brix said the curse might have been blocked due to the magic Charlotte and Marion used to heal me," Jax said. "I might not have even needed them."

She nodded. "That's true, but I didn't want to take any chances."

"I appreciate that," he said, giving her a short nod. "Thank you."

"You're welcome. I really was just trying to keep everyone safe. It's my fault he was targeting you all. If I hadn't gotten involved with him all those years back, if I hadn't had a thing for bad boys, none of this would be happening." She turned to Carson, wincing. "I'm sorry, baby. You're the only good thing that ever came from that situation. You know that, right?"

He gave her a quick nod but turned away, clearly bothered by the direction of the conversation.

"It's not your fault that Phineas is a piece of shit," I said to Trish. "You made a mistake. That doesn't mean you should've had to keep paying the price for years to come.

Dammit, Trish, when you realized he was bad news, you left him. You did everything you could to make sure he was out of your life for good. It didn't work, but that's not on you. It's on him."

She just shrugged and then looked at Ty. "I'm so sorry, baby. Can you forgive me?"

He frowned and then stared at his feet. "I don't know." When he finally looked up, he said, "You should have just told me what was happening. I could have dealt with it. Now I don't trust you. And I'll never get those years back that I've missed out on with Carson."

Before she could reply, he got up and walked back into the house.

Trish wiped a tear away. "He's probably right," she choked out.

"Maybe, but he was just eighteen," I said. "You did what you thought was best. But I'm not going to lie to you, Trish. It hurts. A lot. You left a giant hole in our lives, and while I understand you thought you had no choice, I think we could have handled the truth. Or more importantly, we'd have rather known and dealt with that truth than go through the pain of losing you."

She glanced away and wiped her cheeks again. Then she stood. "I understand." She started to walk away and then stopped. "Jax, you're going to need a pack to navigate this change. You're welcome to join me and my packmate, Dannika, if you want. We'll help you learn what it means to be a wolf."

He stared up at her. "What if I can't shift? Will I still need a pack then?"

She nodded. "Yes. It's not just the shift. It's other

personality changes, urges, and instincts." Trish turned her attention to me. "Navigating this will be a challenge, and I want you to be at your best for Marion. She deserves that."

"I'll think about it," Jax said, reaching out to take my hand in his.

Carson got to his feet. "Will you tell Ty I'll call him, please? I want to give him some time to process all of this before we speak again. I'm sure he's going to have questions."

"I will." I stood and pulled him into a hug. "I'm sorry I doubted you."

He let out a short laugh. "I'd have been concerned if you hadn't."

That made me smile and lifted a load off my heart. Carson appeared to be a good man. He'd be good for Ty once the dust settled.

"Trish?" I called.

She turned to look at me.

"Will you be in touch? With me, I mean?" She'd said Jax could join her small pack, but she hadn't said anything about maintaining any other relationships.

"If you want me to," she said. "I know I hurt you."

"You did, but only because I love you. If you ghost me again, I'll never forgive you."

Tears fell down her cheeks and without another word, she engulfed me in a hug. As we stood there, years of grief seemed to dissipate into the ether. We weren't going to solve all our differences in one evening, but Trish was back, and that was all that really mattered.

CHAPTER 27

A week later, I was sitting at my desk in the office enjoying the fresh energy. The coven had stopped by, and we'd smudged the place, cleansing it of the negative energy that had been left behind by Trace's curse. Things had been quiet as I worked to try to come up with a plan to reestablish Miss Matched as the premier dating service for people looking for love after forty. It was a challenge, but that was fine. I'd been through worse before.

The door opened and Sara Groveland walked in. She looked tired and as if she'd aged ten years. My heart ached for her and everything she'd gone through over the past few weeks. I stood. "Sara, hi. I wasn't expecting you today."

"I know. I just wanted to stop by and offer my apologies. None of this would have happened if I hadn't trusted some stranger on the internet." Her eyes were puffy, and her hair was pulled back into a messy ponytail. Not the kind that was stylish messy. The kind that looked like she hadn't brushed her hair in a few days and couldn't be bothered to even try.

"Hey," I said, offering her a chair. "It's not your fault." She really had no idea just how wrong she was about her assessment. Nor could I tell her that Trish's ex had blown into town, intending to scam anyone and everyone who had more than a couple of nickels to rub together. "You didn't ask for any of this. Trusting people isn't a flaw."

She guffawed. "It's not exactly smart though, is it?"

I hated that she was blaming herself. "Sara—"

"No. Never mind. This isn't who I am." She sat up straight in her chair, her shoulders back. "I will not let some tiny, piece-of-shit man beat me down. You're right. I didn't ask for this. All I wanted was a nice man to go out on dates with who enjoys farm-to-table restaurants and hiking in the woods. Is that too much to ask?"

"Not in the slightest," I said. "In fact, if you ever decide to give it another go, I'm sure I can find you someone exactly like that."

She inhaled sharply. "I'm not ready. I wish I could say I was, but Andrew did a number on me. I'm glad he's behind bars. He deserves a swift kick in the nuts, but prison is fine, too."

I chuckled. "Wouldn't that be nice if the judge lined up all the jackholes who try to take advantage of us and let us kick them where it counts?"

"I'd vote for it." She gave me a small smile and then stood. "I'm sorry. I didn't mean to come and cry on your shoulder. I really just wanted to apologize and thank you for your help. I really wish I'd have gone with your recommendation and hired Sebastian. He's such a lovely man. I don't know what I ever saw in that jerk Andrew."

"Scammers make their living by charming their victims," I said.

She visibly shuddered. "I hate that word, *victim*. It just makes me feel so dumb."

"I'm sorry. I know what you mean. Still, the sentiment is the same. He's good at what he does. That's the only reason he hasn't been caught before."

"I guess. It's going to take me a long time to trust again." She ran a hand down her face. "Ugh. I hate everything right now."

"I heard you got a contract to supply the new restaurant they're opening up next door. That's good news," I said.

Her eyes lit up, and I was happy I'd brightened her mood. "Yes. It's a Thai place. I can't wait to try the pumpkin curry. I heard it's delicious."

We chatted for a few more minutes about the new restaurant before Sara said, "I better go. I have an appointment to get this hair done down at the Liminal Space Day Spa. I hear they can work magic. We'll see. If they can do something with this mess, then maybe they're right."

I assured her that I had confidence they would and then added, "When you're ready to try the dating scene again, give me a call. We'll make sure you find the perfect match."

"I'm not sure I'll ever be ready, but if you want to help me find the perfect puppy, then you're hired," she said with a little smile.

"You're on. Puppies for the win." I walked her to the door, and as she was leaving, Iris blew in.

"You're not going to believe this. I think I've found the

answer to all this terrible publicity." She flung herself into the leather chair that sat opposite my desk.

I raised my eyebrows at her. "Well, are you going to make me beg, or are you going to tell me this awesome news?"

"You are going to love me forever." Iris sat up and preened and then laughed at herself. "Well, you're probably going to love *Carly* forever, but I'm the one who asked her for suggestions, so I'm taking the credit."

"Oh. My. Gods! Just spit it out already," I said with a laugh.

"Have you met Autumn? The woman who is opening the pottery studio around the corner?" Iris asked, her eyes twinkling with mischief.

"Yeah, I ran into her at the café earlier this week. Nice lady. She said she was going to start offering classes. I've always wanted to learn to throw pots."

"Yeah, me too. But do you know *who* she is?"

"Autumn Winters?" I asked, perplexed. "So?"

"No, Marion. I mean yes, that's her legal name, but her stage name is Autumn Faye. As in the Autumn Faye who was on that hit television show twenty years ago. The one that still plays on all the streaming stations. She's agreed to be your next client. If it all goes well, she told Carly she'd do an interview about her experience to help you out. Turns out, she's all about small business now and is very interested in making sure we have a vibrant downtown area."

I sat back, stunned. "She agreed to that? Why?"

"Because we're become friends. It helps that she's friends with Carly too, and she said any friend of Carly's is a friend of hers. This is exactly what we needed to put a fresh face on this agency." Iris beamed, looking very pleased with herself.

I chuckled. "You do realize it's Carly who deserves the credit for this, right?"

Iris waved an unconcerned hand. "Whatever. I'm the one who asked her if she had any friends who need a date, so I deserve something."

I stood, walked over to her, and pulled her out of her chair to give her a giant hug. "You're the best. You know that, right?"

"I have my moments."

I grabbed my keys. "Let's go check out the new pottery shop. I think I might need a vase or two."

"Wow. Someone did a little bit of retail therapy," Charlotte said from her spot on the couch. Denver was sitting opposite her, and there was a stack of cards between them.

"Playing Go Fish again?" I teased.

"Please. It's all-out war with blackjack. I'm winning. Denver owes me five back massages, two fancy dinners, and a trip up the coast."

"Something tells me Denver isn't really trying that hard." I glanced at him. "Hey."

He chuckled. "Hi, Marion."

"He's trying!" Charlotte called after me as I made my way into the kitchen to drop off my new vase. The visit with Autumn had been more than productive. Not only had I signed up for classes to learn to make pottery, we'd also made an appointment for her to come in and talk about what she wanted out of a partner. It'd been a win for both of us. Then I put a giant dent in my credit card when I fell in love with a fiery red vase that reminded me of Jax's aura when we were together. The movement of the design was just full of passion, and I wasn't able to pass it up.

The front door opened, and familiar footsteps sounded on the hardwood.

"She's in the kitchen," I heard Charlotte call.

A moment later, Jax walked up behind me and wrapped his arms around my waist. He pressed a soft kiss to my neck. "Hey, gorgeous."

"Hey," I said, leaning back against him, loving the feel of his rock-solid body. "What brings you here this early?" Normally he'd still be at work for another couple of hours.

"I wanted to see if you'd take a drive with me."

I turned to look up at him. "Where?"

He brushed a lock of hair out of my eye and tucked it behind my ear. "Out to the cove."

I grinned up at him. "I'm in. Ready now?"

He nodded, and together we walked out to his truck.

Jax was quiet on the ride over to his little piece of paradise. But he'd been on the quieter side ever since our meeting with Trish. Brix had stopped by that same evening and had confirmed Trish's story and informed us that Phineas's gang of scammers had all been apprehended and that all charges against Sara were going to be dropped. Everything had mostly been wrapped up with a neat little pin.

Sort of, anyway. Ty was still angry at his mom for lying to us. For the moment, he didn't want to talk to her. But he was talking to Carson, and the two were trying to build a relationship. Mostly, they didn't talk about Trish because Ty was still processing everything. I knew that someday soon, he'd get to a place where he was ready to talk with her again, but right now, he was just too hurt. If there was one thing Ty couldn't handle, it was being abandoned. His father had done it before he was even born. And whether he acknowledged it or not, that had deeply affected him. Plus there was the fact that he was questioning her version of events about his father. She'd been dishonest about so many things, he just didn't know what to believe anymore.

He'd never had very much family. Losing Trish had been a blow he hadn't quite recovered from. Learning the one person he'd always trusted had walked away from him had severely wounded him. Honestly, I was fairly positive he'd always wear those scars.

Jax parked next to the small trailhead and led me by the hand to the beach. The sun was just starting to set over the water, and I had it in my mind that this was going to be some sort of romantic date. But as our feet hit the sand, he stuffed his hands into his pockets and lowered his head as we walked toward the water, making it look like he had something on his mind.

"What is it, Jax?" I said, stopping when I got to the surf.

He glanced up, a pained expression on his face.

"Whoa. You're not breaking up with me, are you?"

When he didn't say anything, I took a step back, putting more distance between us. My lungs were constricting, and I seemed to be having trouble breathing. "Jax?" I forced out. "Say something. Are you breaking up with me?"

"No," he said with a slow shake of his head. "But after you hear what I have to say, it might be you who leaves me."

I pressed a hand to my heart, trying to keep it from beating right out of my chest. At least I could breathe again. "Why don't you let me be the judge of that?"

"Right." He kicked his shoes off and rolled up his jeans.

I followed his lead, and then together we walked through the gentle surf. When he reached out for my hand, I clasped on tight and said, "You better start talking. My mind is racing with all kinds of terrible things."

"Sorry," he said, squeezing my fingers. "I didn't mean to be so dramatic. This is just… hard."

I didn't pretend to understand what he was going through. He'd been bitten by a wolf and was now cursed. He'd spent the last week trying to decide whether he was going to eat the cookie elixirs for the rest of his life to make sure he never shifted or if he was going to explore his shifter side and see if that was even an option.

He'd been restless and moody, though never mean. Just… different. I knew it weighed on him. He wasn't himself, and he was having trouble adjusting to the new Jax.

"I've made a decision," he said.

"Okay." I let out the breath I'd been holding and turned to face him, taking his other hand so that both were occupied. "This sounds like a decision I'm not going to like."

"I doubt you will." He grimaced. "Honestly, I'm not fond of the choice either, but I feel like I have to do this. In order to give you all of myself, I need to figure out exactly who I am now. I don't think I can do that here, pretending that nothing has changed."

"You're leaving," I said flatly.

"It's not forever."

We just stared at each other, neither of us knowing what to say.

"For how long?" I finally asked.

"As long as it takes, I guess." He raised my left hand and kissed it. "I love you, Marion. The only thing I've ever truly wanted in this life is you. You know that, right?"

"No," I said with a startled laugh. "I mean, you've wanted other things. A good career, friendship. And a nice truck," I added as a joke.

His lips twitched in amusement. "Sure, those things are nice, but if I had to choose, you'd win every single time."

"Except this time," I said, frowning. "Are you sure you have to leave to go find yourself... or whatever?"

He swallowed and I knew this was hurting him just as much as it was hurting me. "This is just something I have to do. I don't... I can't..." He closed his eyes. "I need to get a handle on whatever has a hold over me. Or at least figure out how to accept it. Then I'll come right back here to this spot. To you and the home I promised to build you."

Tears pricked the backs of my eyes. I didn't bother to blink them back. While I knew that he believed every word he was saying, for some reason, I felt like I was losing him all over again. "You're taking Trish up on her offer?"

He nodded.

"Will I hear from you?" I asked.

"No. Not at first at least." He paused and then added, "I spoke to Hollister."

"You did?" The words came out high-pitched and full of surprise.

He let out a soft chuckle. "I know. It's a shock. But I needed advice and like you always say, he knows everything. He told me that new werewolves need time to settle into their skin. Being around humans can be disorienting and actually impede the transition. And in a lot of cases, it can ruin relationships. Especially with those we're closest to. I can't let that happen. So I'm going, and when I'm whole again, I'll come back for you. If you're willing to wait for me, that is. I'll understand if—"

I pressed my lips to his, cutting off his words. When I pulled away, I said, "I'll be here. No matter how long it takes."

He let out a relieved sigh. "Trish said she'll be in touch with you. She'll be able to get messages to me if you need me."

I wanted to tell him that I always needed him, but I understood what he was saying and respected his decision. This was his change. His ordeal. However he needed to deal with it, I'd support him. "When are you leaving?"

"Now." He glanced toward the tree line. Just in the distance, I spotted a smallish gray wolf waiting for him.

The tears were streaming down my face when he bent his head and kissed me. Then he was gone.

I didn't remember the drive home. All I knew was that I'd somehow managed to get Jax's truck back to my place, and when I walked in, Charlotte was waiting for me.

"Brix called," she said, holding out my dagger. "He needs us."

I stared at the dagger and then nodded once. "Let's go."

DEANNA'S BOOK LIST

Witches of Keating Hollow:
Soul of the Witch
Heart of the Witch
Spirit of the Witch
Dreams of the Witch
Courage of the Witch
Love of the Witch
Power of the Witch
Essence of the Witch
Muse of the Witch
Vision of the Witch
Waking of the Witch
Honor of the Witch
Promise of the Witch
Return of the Witch
Fortune of the Witch

Keating Hollow Happily Ever Afters:

Gift of the Witch
Wisdom of the Witch

Witches of Befana Bay:
The Witch's Silver Lining

Witches of Christmas Grove:
A Witch For Mr. Holiday
A Witch For Mr. Christmas
A Witch For Mr. Winter
A Witch For Mr. Mistletoe
A Witch For Mr. Frost

Premonition Pointe Novels:
Witching For Grace
Witching For Hope
Witching For Joy
Witching For Clarity
Witching For Moxie
Witching For Kismet

Miss Matched Midlife Dating Agency:
Star-crossed Witch
Honor-bound Witch
Outmatched Witch
Moonstruck Witch
Rainmaker Witch

Jade Calhoun Novels:
Haunted on Bourbon Street
Witches of Bourbon Street

Demons of Bourbon Street
Angels of Bourbon Street
Shadows of Bourbon Street
Incubus of Bourbon Street
Bewitched on Bourbon Street
Hexed on Bourbon Street
Dragons of Bourbon Street

Pyper Rayne Novels:
Spirits, Stilettos, and a Silver Bustier
Spirits, Rock Stars, and a Midnight Chocolate Bar
Spirits, Beignets, and a Bayou Biker Gang
Spirits, Diamonds, and a Drive-thru Daiquiri Stand
Spirits, Spells, and Wedding Bells

Ida May Chronicles:
Witched To Death
Witch, Please
Stop Your Witchin'

Crescent City Fae Novels:
Influential Magic
Irresistible Magic
Intoxicating Magic

Last Witch Standing:
Bewitched by Moonlight
Soulless at Sunset
Bloodlust By Midnight
Bitten At Daybreak

Witch Island Brides:
The Wolf's New Year Bride
The Vampire's Last Dance
The Warlock's Enchanted Kiss
The Shifter's First Bite

Destiny Novels:
Defining Destiny
Accepting Fate

Wolves of the Rising Sun:
Jace
Aiden
Luc
Craved
Silas
Darien
Wren

Black Bear Outlaws:
Cyrus
Chase
Cole

Bayou Springs Alien Mail Order Brides:
Zeke
Gunn
Echo

ABOUT THE AUTHOR

New York Times and USA Today bestselling author, Deanna Chase, is a native Californian, transplanted to the slower paced lifestyle of southeastern Louisiana. When she isn't writing, she is often goofing off with her husband in New Orleans or playing with her two shih tzu dogs. For more information and updates on newest releases visit her website at deannachase.com.